She was Wearing a Froth of Lace and Satin . . .

and his gaze seemed searing as it went deliberately over the deep decolletage of her bodice, lingered on her creamy skin, and then came slowly back to her face. He bent to her abruptly, parting her lips with a hard kiss that demanded and then possessed in turn. Julie could do nothing but surrender to the seeking caresses of his hands and mouth, as his lips blazed a trail downward on her delicate skin. There was not even time to feel nervous or embarrassed at her own uninhibited response. For this was where she'd wanted to be all along—clasped tight in his arms with his lips moving on hers. . . .

Other SIGNET Books by Glenna Finley

* Price slightly higher in Canada

If you wish to order these titles,
please see the coupon in
the back of this book.

THE MARRIAGE MERGER

MERGER

GLENNA FINLEY

Marriage is popular because it combines the maximum of temptation with the maximum of opportunity.
—G. B. SHAW

A SIGNET BOOK

NEW AMERICAN LIBRARY

TIMES MIRROR

SIGNET TRADEMARK REG. U.S. PAT. OFF. AND FOREIGN COUNTRIES
REGISTERED TRADEMARK—MARCA REGISTRADA
HECHO EN CHICAGO, U.S.A.

SIGNET, SIGNET CLASSICS, MENTOR, PLUME and MERIDIAN BOOKS
are published by The New American Library, Inc.,
1301 Avenue of the Americas, New York, New York 10019

First Signet Printing, December, 1978

1 2 3 4 5 6 7 8 9

PRINTED IN THE UNITED STATES OF AMERICA

For Donald

ONE

"Let's have that again—in words of one syllable this time," Robert Holdridge said to the young woman standing in front of his desk.

Julie Randall almost wilted under his glare and had to clear her throat before she could reply. "I just mentioned that my grandfather doesn't think I should go with you next week."

Robert's tone became even more ominous. "And how did he reach that conclusion?"

"I don't know—but he said that in his day a man would have been horsewhipped for suggesting it," she finished in a spurt of defiance.

"For taking a secretary on a business trip?" Her employer stared incredulously back at her. "Good god, what have you been telling him? Or didn't you bother to mention that it wasn't my original intention?"

Julie's glance slid guiltily to his bandaged right hand resting on the desk top. "Of course I did. It didn't make any difference."

"Then I suggest that you go into greater detail the next time you talk to him."

"There's no point in it," she protested. "I explained how important this Far Eastern trip is to the firm and how long you've been planning it. I even told him about your hand—and how I closed the door on it by mistake." Her voice dropped as she remembered that awful day the week before when she'd inadvertently slammed the connecting door between their two offices.

An hour and half later, Robert had come back to the office with a thick bandage on his injured fingers and the terse comment that he'd been ordered to keep his hand immobile until it healed. "Which means that you'll have to come along on this damned Pacific junket, I suppose," he'd growled, showing exactly how he felt about it. "Somebody will have to take notes, and you've effectively put me out of commission."

"I've already apologized," she'd said. She'd been as pale as he was, after waiting for the result of his doctor's visit. Then the important part of his remarks finally penetrated. "But you can't want me along on that trip. Not now," she had finished lamely.

"I didn't say that I did." His tone showed that he knew what she meant by that and how their promising relationship had deteriorated.

When Julie had joined the venerable Los Angeles travel firm of Holdridge and Son a year before, she'd felt that the heavens had opened to signal her triumph at being appointed senior travel associate. Her qualifications on the job application had consisted mainly of a fine arts degree, which was insecure ground when compared with the other candidates for the position. She hadn't realized that her employer also appreciated her unstated but obvious physical assets. These included intelligent gray-blue eyes, thick, soft ash-brown hair pulled back to show a flawless profile, and finally a captivating smile which would melt even the crustiest patron. When these features were added to a trim five foot four inch figure, the resultant package was as deluxe as any offering that

Holdridge and Son had on the tour agenda. Later, when the firm discovered that Julie possessed an uncanny memory for airline schedules and cruise departures, her salary went up like a rocket from the Florida coast. Two months afterward, she ranked as executive assistant to Mr. Holdridge himself—a gray-haired gentleman who treated her with courtly old-world courtesy.

Unfortunately, a mild coronary disorder forced him into early retirement, and he summoned his son and heir apparent back to the head office from his post as director of the company's European operations.

Any adjectives connected with Robert Holdridge included words like "formidable," "determined," or "absolutely absorbed in the business"—which hadn't made Julie look forward to his arrival. One of the firm's feminine travel representatives who'd just returned from the Naples office put it more bluntly. "He couldn't care less about the women in the firm," she reported. "On most weekends, he was off investigating Roman antiquities. Although the day I came home, I saw him at the airport with a blonde who looked more like a refugee from the Cannes Film Festival than a ruin from Carthage. She was wearing a gorgeous poplin raincoat lined in opossum straight from St. Laurent's new collection."

"Or maybe Mr. Holdridge's collection," Julie had observed tartly. "He's only thirty-two or three and a bachelor."

The other had looked at her with amusement. "I see his personnel file has gotten around."

"Don't be silly. His father just happened to mention it one day. Something about hoping

Robert would settle down and think about getting married when he came home."

"From the way Robert was looking at that blonde in the airport, marriage was the last thing on his mind. It's a pity he doesn't believe in mixing business and pleasure. And he doesn't, you know, so don't get any ideas about his unbending with the hired help."

Julie had remembered the warning. She was so intent on not giving her new employer the wrong impression that she wore a severely tailored suit for a solid week after his arrival and drank her coffee black when he poured it at their morning conferences because she was afraid to ask for cream.

She had softened slightly by the next week because her new employer had turned out to be an extraordinarily appealing man. He had a penetrating gray-eyed gaze and straight dark brown hair which was usually rumpled and falling over his forehead because he ran an absent hand through it when concentrating on his work. He was tall—although not overly so—and lean, but not so lean that she wasn't aware of broad shoulders under his impeccably tailored sports jackets and suit coats.

For a man ostensibly dedicated to his work, he had not been slow to note Julie's finer qualities. Only four days elapsed before he took her to lunch, saying that it would be a good chance to discuss the current cruise schedules.

Two days after that, he'd thought it would be appropriate to discuss tour packages over dinner. The following week he invited Julie for a Sunday afternoon at the beach and when she'd hesitantly asked if she should bring a pad and pencil, he'd grinned and said only if she planned to do some sketching.

With that, Julie had stopped shilly-shallying and started enjoying their developing relationship. Robert teased her and laughed with her on their dates, but he limited any physical advances to a thorough but still proper kiss when they parted. The thoughtful glint in his eyes after such leavetakings made Julie think that he was holding himself severely in check since their desks were just an office apart and they worked closely during each business day.

She could understand the wisdom of his actions, but she also knew that the way things were progressing, a chaste kiss wasn't going to suffice for either of them much longer. The anticipation of that day brought a lilt to her voice that didn't go unnoticed among her friends.

The circumstances were in that promising state when Geoff Clarke, an amiable travel consultant, lingered by her desk one afternoon. He was still feeling the effects of a festive farewell luncheon before transferring to a Holdridge overseas post. Cornering Julie behind her typewriter, he managed to give her a drawn-out good-by kiss. She surmised that he'd done the same to every woman along the corridor, so she didn't struggle, knowing that he'd soon stagger on his way.

Robert emerged from his office just in time to see the last of the embrace and Julie's unprotesting part in it. His expression went rapidly from astonishment to frozen distaste as he noted her flushed countenance.

She tried to smooth her hair, wishing she hadn't turned bright red with embarrassment under his surveillance. "Geoff was just telling me good-by," she managed to say.

Geoff hiccuped audibly, not helping their cause. "Allus like to say good-by to Julie," he informed Holdridge. "She's a wonnerful girl—wonnerful."

"Go say good-by to the others," Julie told Geoff, giving his rotund figure an urgent nudge toward the corridor, as Robert remained riveted in the doorway. "Otherwise you'll miss your plane."

Julie's words didn't speed Geoff on his way as she'd hoped. Instead, he managed to drape a heavy arm over her shoulders and pull her around to confront their employer. "That's why I love this girl," Geoff informed him. "Julie really cares about a man. Deserves everything she gets."

"I'll be sure to remember," Robert said as he turned back toward his office. "Now—if you'll excuse me—I have more important things to do."

His smoldering tone made the color drain from Julie's cheeks. "Oh, please—you don't understand," she said. "Did you want me for something?"

Holdridge's eyebrows went up slightly, showing such disdain that Julie took an instinctive step backward even before he said coolly, "Want you, Miss Randall? I'm afraid not," and closed his office door behind him.

Julie's stricken features managed to penetrate Geoff's befuddled mind. "Whatsamatter with him?" Without waiting for an answer, he patted her shoulder and moved toward the hall. "Pay no 'tention to old Rob. He's just jealous. Better get outta here before he comes back," he muttered and lurched out of the office.

Julie stayed where she was, her mind stunned

by Robert's reaction. The obvious remedy was to knock on his door and make him listen to a simple explanation, but she'd only taken a step toward the closed office when she pulled up. It was absurd to explain something so harmless. Robert was the one who should apologize—and probably would as soon as he thought it over.

She glanced at her wristwatch and then tidied the papers on the top of her desk, expecting his closed office door to open at any minute. If he emerged looking suitably sheepish, she would be generous in her forgiveness. He hadn't known that Geoff Clarke started kissing every woman in sight after the second martini.

Julie lingered at her desk until after five and then left the office with her chin up. Probably it was better to discuss the matter after Robert's temper had cooled overnight. She *did* wish that they'd made a date for dinner, but Robert had mentioned earlier that some old family friends were visiting from out of town.

She went home and spent the evening near the telephone just in case he found a chance to call. Unfortunately the phone remained obstinately silent.

Sleep proved elusive and the next morning Julie was at her desk a good half hour early. She had made a thorough hash out of a travel itinerary for one of the most valued Holdridge clients by the time Robert emerged from the elevator, and she was in such a state of misery that she almost threw herself sobbing on his chest.

His impassive glance immediately congealed such heated impulses and she sank weakly back into her desk chair, appalled at her thoughts. The object of them would have gone by with a businesslike "Good morning" if she hadn't instinctively touched his sleeve as he passed.

"Robert." There was a wealth of appeal in the word, but he ignored it, looking at her without any emotion in his face. Julie straightened her shoulders. "I've been waiting to talk to you—to explain," she said.

His thick eyebrows drew together. "Explain what?" The words hung in the air, emphasizing the great gulf between them.

Julie took a deep breath, wondering if this sudden nightmare would ever end. The warm, thoughtful man she'd known had turned overnight into a frightening stranger.

"I said—explain what?" he repeated with awful patience.

"About yesterday. When Geoff was in here—" She plunged on, aware suddenly of how thin her defense would sound. "It wasn't what it looked like."

"You mean he wasn't kissing you?"

"Well, yes—of course he was kissing me," she replied in some confusion.

"Then why should I discuss a personal matter which could only conceivably be of interest to you and Geoff Clarke? Now if you have that trade tour itinerary ready, I'd like to go over it. I have a date for lunch and I want the details settled before I leave." He looked at his watch before letting his impersonal gaze meet hers again. "Is there anything else, Miss Randall?"

The last two words were deliberate and both of them knew it. It was as if he'd unfurled a banner proclaiming a brand-new, strictly business relationship between them. Apparently he'd chosen to blot out everything else because of a foolish, stupid misunderstanding.

Her lips tightened as another possibility occurred to her. He might have been looking for a convenient excuse. Stricken by that possibility, she adopted his coldly polite tone. "No, there's nothing else, Mr. Holdridge. That tour itinerary is already on your desk." Her telephone rang at that moment, giving her a chance to turn away. When she hung up the receiver a minute later, he'd disappeared into his office.

If Julie needed any further proof that their friendship was a thing of the past, it was furnished by a *soignée* brunette who appeared promptly at noon and announced that Mr. Holdridge was expecting her. From the way she clung to his arm when they waited for the elevator a few minutes later, it wasn't going to be a dull business lunch.

Her presence brought Julie's anger out of its dormant state and she accepted a long-standing cocktail date with the representative of a French airline, making sure that he appeared when Robert was leaving that afternoon.

In the days that followed, the two of them exchanged cool, civil greetings and held business meetings that were remarkable for brevity and barely-covered hostility. Julie was thinking seriously of asking for a transfer to the Buenos Aires office even before Robert announced his inspection trip of Far East operations.

It was that day when she compounded all her felonies by closing the door on his hand and forced his reluctant decision to take her with him. "Those damned arrangements were almost impossible to make in Sumatra," he said, "and I've just gotten confirmation on my appointment with the government tourist board in Jakarta. It's too late for cancellations now." He bestowed an annoyed but considering look on Julie's waiting figure. "That's the only reason you're going along."

"I couldn't," she gasped.

"Why not? It's certainly not out of line to expect you to do the work you're paid for. This wouldn't be the first foreign junket you've taken since you were hired."

"Of course not," she snapped back. "But you're still going, aren't you?"

"Naturally."

"And the hotel reservations were for just one room?"

"You should know," he pointed out in an icy tone, "since you made most of them."

"It was all I could get. There's a shortage of tourist accommodations at this season," she replied. "I don't intend to go with you under those conditions."

He stopped so suddenly that she almost ran into him. "Why not? You're certainly safe as far as I'm concerned," he said, looking down his nose at her unhappy face. "Naturally we'll try to make additional hotel arrangements when we arrive."

"You could hire a secretary on the spot. . . ."

His expression became even more forbidding. "Don't be ridiculous. This calls for another Holdridge employee. I've arranged to visit some sites of old civilizations in Sumatra and Java on my own. You can tour with local travel officials for that time if you want. It doesn't have to be decided now." He paused halfway into his office. "We'll leave on schedule the first of the week. Make sure that your health card is up-to-date—

there's cholera in Japan and on parts of the mainland right now. And call Miss Flynn for me and say that I can't pick her up until seven tonight."

Julie had watched the door close behind him with murder in her eye. Miss Flynn was the brunette, and there was nothing in the Holdridge Employees Manual which necessitated making such phone calls. That prompted her to leave a message for the woman saying Mr. Holdridge would be late—without explaining further.

The next morning, Robert didn't let her vagueness pass unnoticed, which showed that Miss Flynn hadn't let his belated arrival go unmentioned.

Heartened by that victory, Julie prepared for the next skirmish. She announced her family's objection to her accompanying him across the Pacific.

She hadn't gotten the words out of her mouth before the Holdridge heavy artillery was wheeled into place. "That doesn't alter the issue!" Robert's statement brought her back to the present in a hurry. "I'm sorry that your grandfather doesn't approve. If you like, I'll phone him and explain things more fully."

"It won't do any good—his mind's made up. And since he's the only family I have, I think it will be simpler all around if I just resign. I hope a month's notice is sufficient." She brought her hand from behind her back and put a typewritten notice on the desk in front of him.

Robert scowled down at the offending document and then raised his head. "Quite sufficient. Provided you're working it out in the Far East with me. Otherwise, I'll institute legal action, which won't help your future career."

She threw out her hands despairingly. "You don't understand. I simply can't go with you. It may not make sense to either of us—but I can see my grandfather's point of view. In his day, a twenty-three-year-old unmarried woman didn't accompany a man on a trip—no matter what the circumstances."

Robert's intent gaze didn't falter. "You mean, he would approve if we had a marriage license in the luggage?"

Her chin went up. "Yes—strange as it seems. But there's no need to make fun of his ideas."

"I'm not doing anything of the kind. Apparently matrimony is the only solution that will satisfy both your grandfather's family honor and me." Robert sounded matter-of-fact as he stood up. "These days a marriage ceremony is easy to dissolve. We can take care of that when we get back. I imagine an annulment would be the easiest. Unless your grandfather would object to that, too." He shot her a questioning glance. "Would he?"

"Why, I guess not—at least, I don't think so." Julie's words trailed off in confusion. "You're not serious about this?"

"I certainly am. We'd better go down for the blood tests now or there won't be time for everything before we leave."

"But you can't schedule a marriage like a business merger!" Her voice gained force as she warmed to her convictions. "It's ridiculous! What do you plan to do—cross your fingers at the part about loving and cherishing for the rest of your life?"

His level glance held hers steadily. "My good

girl, you can't have it both ways—even for your grandfather."

Julie wanted to hit him when she saw his amused expression. "I am *not* your good girl . . ." she cut in heatedly.

Robert shrugged. "That part's immaterial. You can inform your grandfather that, however casual our approach to the matrimonial bonds, you'll return to these shores in the same condition that you left them. Presumably unsullied," he drawled.

Her cheeks flamed. "You mean—"

"I mean that you won't have to worry about any romantic overtures on my part. Unless, of course, you want to change the ground rules along the way. In which case, both of us would have to take a hard look at the long-range effects."

"Those were the same words you used at the opening of that branch office last week."

"The same rules apply," he said, recovering quickly. "If more people went into marriage with a logical approach, the success factor would improve."

"You couldn't talk most women into a blind date with that approach—let alone matrimony."

"Are you complaining?" he asked.

"Of course not."

"Good!" He went to the closet and pulled out a topcoat. "Ready to go?"

"You're serious about this?" she asked, her voice sounding strained and uneven.

"Certainly. There's no need to look so upset," he added. "Nothing has to change in your life. You can even take up with Geoff again if he recovers from the flu in time to meet us in Hong Kong. Who knows, you might be the kind of motivation he needs to get up out of bed. For the moment, that is."

"If there are any more remarks like that, you'll be taking to your bed with considerably more than an injured hand," she said, the words falling like chips of ice. "Geoff Clarke is a good friend of mine—that's all."

"In view of his actions, you're using the word loosely." Then, encountering her angry gaze, Robert shrugged and waited to help her on with her coat. "I'll take your word for it. Anyhow, Geoff should be around to brighten your social life in Hong Kong."

Julie stepped aside and smoothed her topcoat collar herself, not wanting to feel Robert's hands on her shoulders in a way that brought back too many hurtful memories. It was an effort to keep her tone as cool as his. "I hope that you'll be able to recruit somebody for *your* social life when we get there. It's too bad that Miss Flynn won't be around."

"Isn't it? Imogene's the impulsive type, though. She might take a notion to fly over and meet us."

"How nice." Julie walked determinedly ahead of him toward the bank of elevators. "This should all work out fine, then. Everybody will be happy—even Grandfather."

It was hard to say without choking. Every instinct she possessed told her that she was heading straight toward disaster as far as her emotions were concerned. If she had an ounce of sense, she'd be clearing her desk and ducking out the side door instead of marching downtown to make things worse.

The marker light above the end elevator lit up

as the door opened. Robert caught her elbow firmly and steered her that way, saying, "With any luck, we can take care of this blood test and I can still manage to make my date for lunch."

Julie was conscious of an empty feeling in the pit of her stomach that had nothing to do with their rate of descent. "Miss Flynn?"

"Uh-huh." Robert sounded just as casual as the elevator doors parted on the garage floor. "There's a lot to be said for the kind of relationship we're contemplating, isn't there? It's going to present a few problems when I tell Imogene though."

Julie throttled her urge to break into hysterical laughter. "It might, at that. Especially if you invite her to meet us in Hong Kong. Of course, I could furnish you with a good-conduct certificate."

"Thank you, but it won't be necessary," he assured her solemnly.

"Then Imogene certainly doesn't have to worry!" Julie snapped. Unfortunately, she almost tripped over a curb as she said it, so she didn't clearly hear Robert's response as he helped to right her. It sounded something like "in a pig's eye," which was so absurd that it didn't bear thinking about. Much less merit a reply.

TWO

Afterward Julie marveled that the arrangements for the ceremony were accomplished with little more effort than a Holdridge Daily Tour to Tijuana. Robert departed for his lunch date without even having to hurry, letting Julie take a taxi back to work.

He didn't comment on Imogene Flynn's reaction to his impending marriage when he returned to the office that afternoon, but the stern set of his jaw indicated that luncheon hadn't been all sweetness and light.

"Would you like me to order flowers for Miss Flynn?" Julie asked him as he passed her desk.

He surveyed her warily. "Why should I send flowers to Miss Flynn after having lunch with her?"

"I thought condolences were in order—or should it be congratulations?"

"If you want to become our resident psychiatrist, you'll have to fill out a new job application. In the meantime, skip the flowers. When I want you to do something like that, I'll let you know."

"You usually do," she said, noisily closing her desk drawer.

"Exactly." He leaned down to check the calendar by her typewriter. "Will Monday noon suit you for the ceremony?"

"What ceremony?" she asked, without stopping

to think. When he just looked at her, she said, "Oh, *that*."

Robert went on as if she hadn't spoken. "One of the judges is a friend of mine and he can do the job in his chambers. I didn't think you'd want a church ceremony under the circumstances."

"No, of course not," she replied slowly.

"You can tell your grandfather that it's just as legal," Robert went on, "and, of course, he's welcome to attend."

"He's visiting with friends in Florida just now, but I'll give him all the details when I phone tonight."

Robert's eyebrows drew together at that. "I wouldn't explain too much," he began. Then, as she stared at him, he concluded with a rush. "Dammit all—there's no need to draw him a blueprint of our arrangement."

"I wasn't going to. His blood pressure would really soar if he knew the truth. Fortunately, he doesn't suspect your motives."

"It's nice to know that somebody in your family respects old-fashioned virtues."

Robert was making a note on his pocket calendar and missed her smoldering look. It was the typical double standard between sexes, she decided. He condemned her when he thought she was spreading her favors around, yet he had barely waited overnight before switching his own attentions to Imogene Flynn.

"We can have lunch after the ceremony," Robert was going on briskly, "and then inspect that new Greek cruise liner in Long Beach in the afternoon. I want to see what they're offering on those short Caribbean cruises in January. You'll still have time to pack that evening since our plane for Okinawa doesn't leave until almost midnight. It's a long flight, so don't leave your jabs until the last minute—especially if you need cholera and typhoid."

"Jabs" were shop talk for inoculations, and the reaction to cholera and typhoid shots was often the worst part of the trip. The added prospect of a sore arm, a headache, and probably a low fever on a sixteen-hour plane trip across the Pacific didn't bear thinking about.

"I can go down to the health department this afternoon, I suppose," she agreed reluctantly, not looking forward to it.

"I would if I were you. Otherwise, you'll be more fit for the last rites than for a wedding trip on Monday night." The stern line of his mouth slanted into an unexpected smile. "There's undoubtedly a moral in that story but let's not dwell on it."

She couldn't help smiling in response. "All right—but if I appear in the judge's chambers carrying calla lilies instead of carnations, you'll get the message."

Her words made Robert's grin vanish as quickly as it had come. "I got your message on that score some time ago and I seldom make the same mistake twice. Now, it might be a good idea if we got some work done." He walked into his office and shut the door firmly behind him.

Julie looked at his closed door with some regret. In view of his distinctly chilly mood, she decided to postpone changing reservations for their hotel rooms until they were on the scene. Not that she anticipated any trouble. Her employer had shown very clearly that he didn't have togetherness in mind.

She wasn't surprised when there was no telephone call from him over the weekend. Since she had the customary reaction to her cholera and typhoid "jabs" and wasn't feeling sociable, it was just as well.

At eight o'clock Monday morning, the phone rang just as she was leaving her apartment. She walked over and reached for the receiver like an apprentice snake handler lifting a diamondback rattler. "Hullo," she said cautiously.

"Julie—is that you?" Robert sounded just as cautious, unlike his usual assured manner.

"Yes, of course."

"Well, it didn't sound like you."

"This is a ridiculous conversation." Nervousness made her tone more brusque than she intended. "Did you want something?"

"I didn't call for a weather report, if that's what you mean. A car will pick you up at your apartment at eleven-thirty," he flared back. "There's no need for you to come to the office this morning. If the people there got wind of what was going on, we wouldn't get any work done anyway."

"I didn't plan to send out a press notice."

"And I'm saying there's no need for you to come in at all. Probably you can use the time for packing. If you felt as rotten as I did this past weekend, you still have plenty of things to do before the flight tonight."

His abrupt change into the warm, pleasant man she'd known at the beginning of their acquaintance was more disconcerting than his aloofness. "You mean that you had to get jabbed for this trip, too?" she asked, wanting to prolong the conversation.

"I certainly did. I thought all I needed was cholera, but the nurse discovered that my typhoid shot had expired last month. My arm still feels like raw meat this morning. It's a good thing we aren't having the kind of ceremony where the bride clings to the groom coming back down the aisle. I'd start swearing the minute you laid a finger on me."

"We'll be a great pair on the plane," she responded ruefully. "Two snarling untouchables stuffed with aspirin."

His voice warmed with laughter. "I thought I was the only one. It's too damned bad that we can't postpone leaving for a day or two, but it would create chaos if we tried. I had a cable from Dane Hamill yesterday to say that he'll meet us when we arrive. I'll tell you about it later."

There was an awkward pause while both of them tried to think of something appropriate to say. Then Robert added, "This is your last chance to back out if you want to change your mind."

Julie drew in her breath sharply. "That applies both ways."

"I still need you along," he replied without hesitation, "so I haven't changed *my* mind. I presume that your grandfather hasn't changed his either."

"Not that I've heard."

Her careful tone didn't go unnoticed. "Poor Julie," he mocked. "Caught between two stubborn men and too much of a lady to stand up for your rights."

"I didn't think my rights were in any danger."

"They're not, if you mean what I think you do. The word 'conjugal' has been dropped from my vocabulary for the time being. Any other questions while we're about it?"

"You were the one who brought the subject up," she reminded him.

"So I've been hoist with my own petard. At least, we've cleared the air, so maybe we can declare a state of peaceful coexistence while we're gone. Okay with you?" His manner didn't indicate that he particularly cared one way or the other.

"Of course," she replied simply, thinking anything would be better than their wary circling since that fateful afternoon of Geoff's affectionate farewell. "Will it be all right if I wear a suit for the ceremony?"

"I have implicit faith in your judgment. I hope you've recovered by then—I've ordered champagne with our lunch and I have no intention of drinking alone."

He hung up without waiting for her to reply and Julie was smiling as she put down her own receiver. At least their relationship had been resolved. Even if they couldn't recapture lost ground, the trip abroad would be tolerable.

She appeared at the judge's chambers quaking with fear, hoping that no one would notice her trembling hands as she clung to her silk envelope purse with its beautiful spray of bronze cymbidium orchids which had been delivered in the middle of the morning. The lovely bronze-green tones of the delicate blossoms which Robert had sent were the perfect complement for her beige silk tussah suit and its green tie blouse. Her clutch at dignity was tenuous, and if anyone had dropped a paper clip while they waited for the judge to appear, she would have collapsed in a heap. As it was, only her breathless voice belied her surface calm.

Robert had been standing on the curb when she arrived, wearing a well-tailored dark gray suit and blue shirt with a conservative striped tie. Most of the women walking by took time for an approving look at his lean tall figure. When Julie finally stepped out of the car, her heartbeat speeded up alarmingly, but she made sure that he wasn't aware of it and merely bestowed a faint cool smile.

Robert matched her greeting, not mentioning that he'd been pacing back and forth for ten minutes like an expectant father, awaiting her arrival. As a result, he was almost brusque when he reached for his intended's elbow and saw her move back abruptly. "What's the matter?" Then he noticed the way she was holding her arm and grinned in comprehension. "Sorry, I forgot about your shots—I'll get on the other side," he said, and proceeded to do so.

Events moved smoothly after that. The ceremony was brief, and the chaste kiss that Robert deposited on her cheek afterward could have been sanctioned by a puritan father. Julie brooded on that while Robert waited for the judge to complete the formalities on their marriage certificate. Then, appalled at the way her thoughts were going, she assured herself that tepid kisses were exactly what she wanted.

Robert came up beside her as she reached that laudable conclusion. "What are you looking so unhappy about?" he wanted to know. "Anybody would think I was beating you already."

"Very funny." She made an effort to shed her gloomy feelings as she walked into the corridor with him. "Sorry, I felt a little overcome for a minute."

He nodded understandingly as they waited for the elevator. "I had a few bad moments myself. God knows how people ever survive big weddings."

"I suppose couples feel differently about the ceremony if they really want to get married," Julie went on, behaving like a toothache victim who keeps probing to see if the cavity is still there.

Robert looked down at her dispassionately. "Don't get any ideas about that ceremony not being 'real.' In case your grandfather has any doubts, it was just as legal as the half-hour kind in a cathedral." He broke off as the elevator doors opened and didn't say any more until they reached the ground floor. "Are you going to call him right away?"

"I planned to phone him tonight just before we left. Why?"

"It's just conceivable that he might be interested." Robert saw their hired car waiting at the curb and motioned for the driver to stay behind the wheel as he opened the rear door. "We might as well go to lunch in style, and later on, I can drop you off at your apartment," Robert announced when they were on their way to the restaurant.

"What about the Greek cruise ship at Long Beach?" she asked, remembering his plans.

"What about it?"

"I thought we were going to inspect it this afternoon. You mentioned it earlier."

"Oh, that." He stirred on the limousine seat as

if trying to find a more comfortable position. "There's no need for you to come along."

She turned to face him more squarely. "You don't have to be worried about introducing me—if that's the trouble. I've decided not to change my name just for a few weeks."

Robert wasn't impressed by her proclamation. "You can call yourself the Queen of the Night if you want to," he said, "but when you travel with me, you'll be introduced as my wife. As for this afternoon, you've been aboard Greek cruise liners before and I thought you'd rather rest at home before an all-night flight. You look as if you could use it."

His scrutiny brought a wave of color to her face. "I'm sorry," she murmured. "I seem to be making an awful hash of things."

"Relax." Robert patted her hand on the seat between them. "You'll feel better after some food." His eyes narrowed as his glance raked her again. "Did you have any breakfast?"

"A little . . ." she began, and then confessed, "Just coffee—I wasn't hungry."

"Good god, I thought you had more sense. Well, you're going to eat some lunch even if it chokes you."

She started to laugh despite herself. "You sound more like a Victorian father laying down the law than a bridegroom."

"That's your fault. I've never made a woman lose her appetite before. At least, I don't think I have."

"Don't worry, I intend to eat my way through the menu at lunch," she said as the driver drew up to the curb of an imposing office building. "I've heard wonderful things about this roof restaurant."

An express elevator whisked them to the twenty-fifth floor, where the doors opened onto a foyer decorated in shades of brown. A hovering maitre d' greeted Robert with, "Your table is ready, Mr. Holdridge," and led them to a secluded corner table alongside floor-to-ceiling windows tinted in a restful amber shade. Thick plantings of greenery enhanced the decor and served double duty as space dividers in the room. A waiter was already holding a comfortable leather chair for Julie to sink into as they reached their table.

Julie nodded approvingly after he left them with mammoth menus to scan. "All this and delicious food, too, from what I've heard."

"Then make sure that you get some of it inside you," Robert said, frowning as he looked at her across the table. "You've lost weight recently, haven't you?"

Julie shrugged, unwilling to admit that his attitude had ruined her appetite. "Maybe we've both been working too hard. You look as if you've shed a pound or two, as well."

"Could be." He opened his menu and changed the subject. "I told them to bring the champagne first thing. That should help things along."

She noticed that Robert didn't enlarge on what "things" he meant. Apparently he wasn't finding their new relationship easy either. "Neither fish nor fowl," she murmured, unaware that she'd said it aloud.

"I beg your pardon?"

"I said," she repeated clearly, "that we're neither fish nor fowl. It's hard to know how to behave—after this morning," she concluded awkwardly.

The wine waiter appeared just then with their champagne and there was a lull while he performed the uncorking ceremony and filled their stemmed glasses.

Robert lifted his after the man left, surveying the bubbles in the golden liquid. "I thought we weren't going to let that piece of paper make any difference."

"Marriage certificates always make a difference." She lifted her own glass. "Cheers!"

"Cheers!" He returned the salute automatically. "I don't see why anything's different," he continued. "Your grandfather was the one calling the signals."

"I wish you wouldn't keep dragging him into it."

"It's a little hard to keep him out—all things considered."

Julie was staring at her champagne, admiring the sparkling liquid against the sunlight. "I wonder if he had any problems with Grandmother."

"I doubt it." Robert met her stare squarely. "You wouldn't be around to talk about it if he had. For lord's sake, let's eat before we get in any more trouble. What sounds good?"

"Arsenic" was on the tip of her tongue, but she clamped down on it and murmured "Eggs Benedict" when the hovering waiter appeared at Robert's elbow to take their order.

He had no sooner gathered their menus and left before the maitre d' swept up. "Mr. Holdridge—there's a telephone call for you. Will you take it in the foyer?"

Robert nodded and excused himself to Julie. "Sorry, I won't be long."

She frowned as she watched him go, and then made herself concentrate on the busy metropolis on view beyond the big windows. It was a sunny day and unusually clear for southern California. A big jet heading toward the Pacific left a vapor trail across the cloudless sky like a thin ruling line on a mammoth blueprint. Watching it, she tried to decide if the strange feeling in her stomach came from champagne or the prospect of heading west on a similar airplane that night with a husband by her side.

She was jolted out of her reverie by Robert's reappearance at their table. As he pulled out his chair, he looked more like an irritated employer than a beaming bridegroom. "What's wrong?" she asked, aware that those two words constituted a major share of her vocabulary recently. "You seem upset."

He sat down and reached for his wine glass with an angry gesture. "Dammit, you'd be upset, too. I just heard that the air traffic controllers in France are scheduling a 'slowdown' the last part of the week. It'll upset flight operations all over Europe. You know what that will do to the people we have on the continent."

She grimaced as she thought about it. "There are five Holdridge tour groups in Europe now—all scheduled to come home by air in the next week or so. Can our Paris and Rome offices cope with all of them?" she asked, knowing what his answer would be.

"I hope so." He took a swallow of champagne and then leaned back with a sigh. "But I'd better go over and make sure. I'll catch up with you as soon as I can."

Her eyes widened. "You mean that you want me to go to the Far East without you?"

"That's not the way I'd put it," he replied drily, "but it'll do. I was going to tell you about another change in our itinerary when we got on the plane tonight, but this has forced my hand. We have passage booked on one of the Marden Line freighters—the *Anging Mamiri*—sailing from Okinawa to Sumatra via Singapore."

"I thought we were flying for the whole trip."

"Well, we're not," he assured her, "so make plans accordingly."

"*Anging Mamiri*—it sounds like something on an oriental menu. I thought Marden was an American steamship company."

"It is. This ship plies between San Francisco and Indonesia, so the company officials chose an Indonesian name for it. *Anging Mamiri* means 'gentle breeze' in one of the native dialects there. Casey told me about it when I asked."

Julie put down her champagne glass and rubbed her forehead. "I knew I shouldn't have had champagne on an empty stomach." She met his eyes despairingly. "Who in the dickens is Casey?"

Robert reached across the table and gently folded her fingers around the stem of her glass. "It's okay. You haven't cracked up. Casey Waring is head of the Marden line. He and Laurel, his wife, are old friends of mine who live in San Francisco."

"So that's how you were able to wangle space on the ship. Reservations on their freighters are pure gold—" She broke off as she remembered his previous announcement. "Do we have time to go by ship?"

"We'll make time." He leaned back to permit the waiter to serve their lunch and nodded when another waiter came with coffee. After they'd gone, Robert picked up his fork, but he didn't start eating right away. "I don't plan to spend the rest of my life shuttling around Europe," he told Julie. "With any luck, I should be able to catch up with you on the ship at Singapore. That means you'll only have four or five days at sea from Okinawa. The *Mamiri*'s present schedule has her docking overnight at Singapore before sailing directly to Sumatra the next day." He frowned at her quiet figure. "Aren't you going to eat?"

"I forgot." Julie hadn't realized that he was watching her so closely. She took a hasty bite and then, surprised that anything could taste so good, took another.

Afterward, Robert saw that they both had fresh cups of coffee before going on with his instructions. "You can pick up your plane ticket at the airport tonight when you check in for the flight. Make sure that you have your passport and health card. I'll arrange a bank draft that you can collect when you get to Okinawa."

"That isn't necessary. I already have my traveler's checks," she began, only to have him wave her silent again.

"Don't argue. There isn't time. Take your traveler's checks, but there's no need for you to use them. I'm sorry that I won't be around to see you off, but the office has booked me out to London on the polar flight late this afternoon. Dane Hamill will be at the airport to meet you in Okinawa. He was the one who tipped me off about the Marden freighter in the first place."

She frowned thoughtfully. "I thought Mr. Hamill was quitting our company to go in the export business."

"He is—but I persuaded him to stay on his job for an extra month to give Geoff Clarke time to settle in over there. Dane knows more about Hong Kong and Taiwan than any American in the travel business, so Geoff will have a hell of a time replacing him. If there's any mixup though, and Dane doesn't meet you, contact the Marden representative at their office in Naha."

"Naha being Okinawa?"

"The capital. Three hundred thousand people," he informed her. "Any other questions?"

She shook her head. "From what I've heard about Mr. Hamill, there shouldn't be any problems."

"Have you met him?" Robert asked abruptly.

"No, but I've heard a great deal about him—he must be awfully good at his job. Most of the people in the office think he's terrific."

"He's good, all right," Robert admitted, keeping an impassive expression. "The ones who think he's 'terrific' are female and impressionable. I want you to be forewarned."

Julie was in the process of taking a sip of coffee but she halted with the cup halfway to her lips and then lowered it carefully to the saucer again. "Meaning that I come in that category?" she said after a second's pause.

"There's no doubt about the first part." His masculine gaze lingered deliberately on her snug-fitting blouse. "I'm not sure about the second."

Julie bunched her napkin and slammed it on the

table, as if flinging down a gauntlet. "Are you sure that you don't want to warn Mr. Hamill?"

"It won't be necessary," Robert replied coldly. "He knows that we were being married today. Dane isn't one to get carried away with ideas of romance, illicit or otherwise, if it interferes with business."

"I see." Julie decided that she wasn't going to sit there like a mouse and be insulted just because of a meaningless marriage ceremony. "I presume the same rules apply in my case. Anything goes except in office hours," she said, purposely baiting him.

Robert wasn't drawn into the net. "I have every confidence in your integrity and discretion until I arrive."

"And then?"

"Then there should be no problem at all." He was signing the lunch check as he spoke and waited until the waiter removed it before he stood up. "Shall we go?"

They rode down the elevator in silence. Robert didn't reopen the conversation until they reached the curb where the limousine and driver were waiting. "I'll take a cab back to the office," he said as the driver jumped out to open the door for Julie. "I have a lot of things to do before that plane this afternoon. The driver will pick you up at your place and take you out to the airport tonight."

Robert was treating her like a feather-brained Holdridge client on a first tour and she struggled to keep a straight face. By then, he was saying to the driver. "I want you to get my wife to the airport in plenty of time for the check-in tonight and make sure that there's someone to help with the luggage."

The driver nodded. "Don't worry about it, Mr. Holdridge. It'll be taken care of."

"Well, that's everything then." Robert turned back to face Julie on the sidewalk. He put a proprietary hand at her elbow and she thought he was going to help her into the car until she felt him draw her forward. She glanced up in surprise, but obediently swayed toward him for another token kiss like the one he'd bestowed in the judge's chambers. Her forehead came into contact with his broad chest and she stood there, nose burrowed against his shirt button as she waited for his lips to descend on her brow. When a second or two passed and nothing happened, she opened an eyelid just a smidgin to see what caused the delay. She saw Robert looking down at her, laughter gleaming in his eyes. If he'd ever had any idea of kissing her good-by, it was long gone.

She straightened abruptly, her cheeks flaming at her stupid mistake.

Robert didn't let her linger on it. "There'll be other days," he said, keeping a firm grip on her arm. "In the meantime, don't get the wrong idea."

"I don't know what you mean," she said, striving to regain a modicum of dignity.

His fingers moved down to touch the diamond-studded wedding band he'd slipped on her finger earlier. "The hell you don't," he said mildly. "I'll expect to see you at the rail of the *Mamiri* when she docks at Singapore. Just remember that I keep very good track of my property—no matter where it is."

She yanked her hand out of his, hoping he

didn't notice how her fingers had trembled in his clasp. "You're behind the times, Mr. Holdridge. That's just a certificate in your pocket—not a deed of ownership."

His look of amusement deepened. "Did you take Latin in school?"

She shook her head, bewildered. "What does Latin have to do with it?"

"There's a motto you learn at the very beginning of the course. Something about 'Render every man his due.' In Singapore," he reminded her, "I'll be around to collect mine."

THREE

When the Okinawan landscape finally appeared beneath the wing of the jumbo jet the next morning, Julie was in no mood to appreciate scenic details of the rock-ribbed island. The prospect of standing on solid ground again was the only thing that held any appeal for her just then. Despite advertisements to the contrary, air travel lost any glamour when passengers approached their seventeenth hour in the same thinly upholstered seat.

The first leg of the flight to Honolulu hadn't been bad, but the next segment across the Pacific started to lose its luster after she cooled her heels in the airport to change planes. Hours later, when the aircraft departed Guam, the stewardess announced that it was a day later, courtesy of the date line crossing. The passengers, who were glassy-eyed with fatigue, felt as if they'd actually spent the extra twenty-four hours in pressurized captivity. When the aircraft captain at long last told them of their impending descent at Okinawa, Julie could hardly believe it.

The long flight would have been pleasanter with Robert sitting next to her rather than the overweight businessman bound for Taiwan. He'd boarded at Honolulu, swallowed a sleeping pill, and had only awakened at brief intervals thereafter. "Can't stand flying," he'd complained during one of the intervals and then closed his eyes again.

Julie had spent most of her time staring through the window into the darkness, wondering if Robert was finding his trip as hard to endure. She'd shifted in the cramped seat, wishing that she could sleep like her companion. Unfortunately, she didn't close an eye, so when the Okinawa coastline appeared, she felt as if she'd better move while she still could. She'd stood in line to wash her face and apply lipstick but the result hadn't been entirely successful. The stewardess who came around to check on her seat belt had said sympathetically, "I hope you have reservations if you're staying in Naha for a while. The place is jammed. Crowded conditions in the home islands of Japan have been responsible for the big population migration here."

"I had no idea," Julie murmured, her eyes widening as she stared down at the modern city buildings spread out below them.

"You're not alone. Most visitors think of Okinawa in terms of World War Two, when the place was mainly rocks and caves. Not that Naha is the pleasure port of the Pacific even now. You'd have as much fun spending a weekend in the Aleutians in midwinter." She gave Julie a considering look. "Unless you know somebody on the island to make it worthwhile."

"Not really. I'm catching a ship here for Singapore," Julie confided, happy to talk to someone after the enforced silence of the long flight.

The middle-aged man beside her stirred and sat up, yawning. "Singapore is the place for me. I wish I was headed there instead of Taiwan."

"Right now we're landing at Okinawa, so fasten your seatbelt, please," the stewardess told him and gave Julie a friendly nod before disappearing down the aisle.

The man yawned again and fumbled with the belt to get it around his middle. "I s'pose I missed breakfast," he grumbled to Julie.

She nodded.

"Oh, well—they'll serve juice and rolls when we take off again," he said resignedly. "I could use some coffee, but there's not much in the way of food served in the airport here. Did you say you were catching a freighter?" He was watching her put away some earphones in the pocket of the seat ahead.

She nodded again, amused that he was suddenly so talkative. "An American ship. It should be in the harbor here now."

"God, I envy you. Good food, nothing to do except laze in the sun." His glance flickered over the band on her third finger. "Almost all the comforts of home."

"My husband is joining the ship at Singapore," Julie found herself saying and then blushed as he chuckled.

"I sort of thought he might be. Can't say as I blame him," he said, even as the jet's wheels came down on the long runway. Seconds later the engines whined into reverse power. "I'm glad the pilot knows what he's doing—go off the end of the runway here and we end up in the middle of the harbor. You'd be alongside that freighter sooner than you'd planned."

There was the customary struggle of the passengers to extract their carry-on luggage from under the seats while the plane slowly taxied toward the sprawling terminal buildings. When they braked and the engine noise subsided, a muffled thud showed that stairs had been placed at the exit door. By the time a stewardess announced that Okinawa passengers could deplane and local time was 8:45 A.M., most of the people in the aircraft were filing off.

Julie was amused to see how the quantity of hand luggage varied according to nationality. Japanese returning home had the most—staggering with plastic shopping bags full of duty-free liquor and cigarettes in addition to their carry-on luggage. In-transit travelers going on to Taiwan were sauntering out with their hands in their pockets, while the rest of the passengers carried smaller cases and bundles. Julie pushed her purse strap more securely on her shoulder and picked up her soft-sided tote bag. She nodded her thanks to the pleasant stewardess who stood by the door, went down the steep metal stairway, and walked over to where airport buses waited to carry passengers to the terminal still about two blocks away.

It was a clear sunny morning with just wisps of clouds which the plane had slipped through on its descent. The breeze was forceful enough that the Nipponese jet taking off at that moment on the main runway became airborne within seconds. Its engine noise made the bus windows rattle, and Julie gave up trying to rest her head against the glass as she waited for the coach to fill.

When the bus finally deposited them at the low white terminal building, she walked up the short ramp to where visitors waited in the observation area. At first, all she could see were Japanese families noisily and happily greeting their arriving friends. The young women, in jeans and T-shirts, looked much like their counterparts in

Honolulu. The men, however, wore immaculate suits and shoes with heels and thick soles to add a few more inches to their height. A blue haze of cigarette smoke hung over the visitors' room even that early in the morning.

Julie was moving through the crowd toward the immigration and customs lines when a male voice said, "You must be Mrs. Holdridge. Or can I just call you Julie?"

She turned so quickly that her purse strap slid from her shoulder and her bag slithered downward.

"Here, let me." The fair-haired man who had spoken was beside her in an instant, putting the strap back where it belonged and taking the laden tote bag from her hand. "I'm Dane Hamill," he said with a smile. "You've probably guessed that by now. Welcome to Okinawa." His smile widened sympathetically. "Should I ask how your flight was?"

Julie managed to find a deserted place by a duty-free perfume counter. "Long," she admitted. "Otherwise uneventful—which is the way I prefer them. I hope I haven't kept you waiting."

"Not at all." His masculine glance went over her quickly, the alert expression curiously at variance with his casual manner. He was a fairly tall, thin man in his mid thirties, with high cheekbones and an aquiline nose which gave him an unconsciously disdainful air. The gleam in his eyes promptly belied it, brimming with male magnetism. Julie instantly understood his success with the feminine sex.

"I knew Rob would pick a winner when he got around to matrimony," Dane said as he completed his own appraisal. "I'm just surprised that he let you wander this far on your own. What happened? Did the strain of attending his own wedding send him into shock?"

Julie smiled back at him, grateful for the way he was dispelling her nervousness. "Something like that. Of course, he used the excuse of an air controllers' strike on the continent. He's promised to appear in Singapore though."

"Damn! That's what I was afraid of." Dane shook his head in mock sorrow. "No wonder he trusted me to chaperone you on the *Mamiri*. What can a man do in four or five days?"

"Well, I plan to do as little as possible myself," Julie said, deciding the subject had gone far enough. "Right now, my stomach's still on Honolulu time and I think my brain stopped functioning as soon as we passed Catalina." Her voice trailed off as she thought about his last sentence. "Are you sailing on the *Anging Mamiri* today, too?"

"Why, yes." He sounded amused. "Anything wrong with that?"

"Of course not. Robert didn't mention it—that's all."

"He didn't know. The *Mamiri* just carries four passengers and the couple who had reserved the other suite had to cancel at the last minute. I was in the Marden office when the message came through."

"I see." Julie wondered about his promise to fill in for Geoff but couldn't think of a diplomatic way to mention it.

Dane must have known what she was thinking because he said, "There's a top-flight woman handling things at our office in Taipei. If she has any real problems, she can contact the *Mamiri*. Actually, things will go smoother with her in charge," he confessed. "I had a small run-in with some government officials the other day and if I'd stayed around, they'd probably have revoked my visa. This way, everybody's happy. Shall we go?"

"Of course." Things were moving a little too fast for Julie's weary brain, but she struggled not to show it. She looked around. "I guess Immigration is next for me."

"And the Customs Section is downstairs. I have a car and driver waiting just outside, and when you're cleared—we can go straight to the port. The freighter is scheduled to sail before noon, so there won't be any time for sightseeing, I'm afraid."

"I'll be lucky if I don't fall asleep in the car," she confessed, following him as he led the way to the immigration line.

"You'll have to do this part on your own," Dane told her, putting down the tote bag by her side. "It's only for arriving passengers. I'll see you downstairs by the baggage section when you're finished here."

The Japanese immigration officer perused her passport and visa but waved her on after stamping her papers. Julie followed the serpentine of other passengers as they went down one flight of metal stairs to retrieve their baggage. When it appeared, a porter carried her bags over to the customs officers nearby. They searched them thoroughly and then motioned for Julie to close them again before they put a chalk mark on the side of each one.

"You're all through now," Dane said, appearing promptly beside her. He signaled a waiting porter to take her luggage and said, "This way. It's that tan station wagon at the curb."

Julie looked in the direction he indicated and

saw a standard-sized station wagon with a curtain behind the seats and over the rear windows. In her bemused condition, she thought for a minute that he'd hired a hearse for transport. Then she saw the driver calmly stuffing her luggage in the back section and realized she was letting her imagination go unchecked.

"Anything wrong?" Dane was at her elbow, opening the front door of the car.

"Of course not. I'm impressed with such efficiency," she said. "Where do passengers sit in an Okinawa taxi? Front seat or back?"

"Get in the back unless you like to live dangerously. The people here drive as if they study at kamikaze school to get their licenses."

She got in without another word. The curtain kept her from checking to see if all her luggage was aboard, so she had to take Dane's word for it. He lingered on the curb to give the driver some instructions and then clambered in beside her. "We go through part of the city on the way to the Marden dock, but there's not much in the way of scenery—just freeway and shops." He turned in the seat to smile at her as they started off. "You won't miss anything if you do go to sleep."

"On my first trip to Okinawa!" she exclaimed. "I was just fooling when I mentioned it before. Imagine how many people would like to see this."

"Well, don't get carried away," he replied skeptically. "We don't have many Americans booking return trips. It's pretty tame on landmarks, other than some family tombs that you'll see next to the harbor area."

As the blocks unfolded before them, Julie understood what he meant. If there was one color that predominated on Okinawa, it was gray. Gray pavement, gray sidewalks, and modest gray storefronts with crowded display windows. By then, even the trend of the weather had followed suit. The wispy white clouds in evidence at the airport were making way for their darker relations scudding in from the north.

Dane noted Julie's apprehensive glance at the overcast sky. "I hope you're a good sailor," he said. "The weather report isn't encouraging. That's why our freighter captain may push ahead the sailing time."

"I should think bad weather would delay it instead."

"Not in Okinawa. You'll see what I mean when we get to the harbor. The only protection from the sea at Naha is one small breakwater. If there's a storm and the ocean kicks up, a captain wants to have his ship away from the docks."

Julie failed to find any comfort in the prospect of a typhoon even with acres of empty but angry ocean around, but she didn't let on. Instead she said lightly, "It's a good thing I put in my seasick pills at the last minute. I've heard that these new container ships really roll."

"We may get a chance to find out. With any luck, we'll have smooth sailing by the time we reach Singapore. That husband of yours knew what he was doing."

Julie tried not to jump every time he mentioned Robert in his new role. "What do you mean?"

"This stretch of ocean by Okinawa is one big tropical storm or typhoon. When we sail for Indonesia from Singapore, it's nearly all protected water—recommended for cruise ships and passengers who sail on them. At the prices they're paying, they don't intend to miss a meal while they're at sea. Can't say as I blame them."

"Nor I." Julie decided to skip worrying about the weather. Just then, the promise of stretching out on a stateroom bed was at the top of her priorities. For a while, at least, the bed would be motionless.

"There are those tombs I was telling you about," Dane announced suddenly as the highway curved past a hillside cemetery on the right. He tapped the driver on the shoulder and the man slowed the car's speed obediently. "These vaults have been around for centuries," Dane went on. "Probably of Chinese origin from what we know."

"I've read about them . . ." Julie rolled down the car window so she could see better. "The circular shape of the plot is supposed to represent the human womb, isn't it?"

"That's right. The symbolism of birth and death making all things equal." Dane pointed to an ornamental jardiniere near the center of a cement crypt. "In the past, they'd open the tomb after a year to let the dust scatter and collect the bones—" He broke off as Julie shuddered noticeably. "Sorry. I've lived in this part of the world so long that I forget how Oriental customs can shock Westerners."

"Normally I'm made of sterner stuff. Try me again after a cup of coffee when we get aboard the ship."

A few minutes later, the harbor area came into view at the left. It was extensive, with armed guards patroling the harbor gates and a high wire fence to protect the blocks of warehouses built next to the water.

"There's the *Anging Mamiri*." Dane pointed to a long modern freighter with containers piled high both forward and aft. Alongside they could see huge mechanized loaders shifting cargo on the dock. Their station wagon turned in at another marked gate and stopped next to the uniformed guard on duty. Dane and Julie must have fitted his conception of American tourists, because they were waved on after merely showing their passports. Their driver drove cautiously along a narrow track leading to the *Mamiri* dock.

A rusted car ferry had just tied up ahead of the freighter and was discharging a steady stream of passengers down an ancient wooden gangway. They carried backbreaking basket loads or rope-tied suitcases and were stoically heading for the long walk to the port gate.

"Obviously they're in better shape than I am," Julie murmured as the station wagon moved past. "Surely they didn't come from Yokohama on that rustbucket."

Dane shook his head. "It calls at the islands around here. I'd hate to be sailing on it in bad weather," he added reflectively.

"Lord, yes. I'm glad the *Mamiri* looks solid and dependable." As the station wagon edged around the stacks of metal containers on the dock, she added, "There's an awful lot of activity here. I hope we don't get run down by a forklift or a loading crane before we get on board."

Dane leaned forward to say something to the driver in Japanese. "We'll pull up as close to the end of the gangway as we can," he told Julie as a shipping official came running up to motion them out of the way of a towering loader which went by with its alarm bell sounding. "You go aboard and I'll watch the transfer of our luggage." He pointed toward a uniformed figure standing by a railing two decks above the gangway. "See that man? Take that outside stair and go through the door behind him. According to the deck plan I saw, you should find the Purser's Office there. That's where you get your cabin key." Dane opened the car door as they pulled up.

"But my things . . ." Julie protested with a worried look over her shoulder. "Don't you want me to carry something?"

"Just do as I say. It isn't safe to be here at loading time." Dane was helping her onto the pavement and pulling her out of the way of a speeding forklift even as he spoke. "This is a hardhat area, and we're getting dirty looks right now. Rob wouldn't approve if I let you get skewered on the dock."

"All right—if you insist." She lingered a moment longer, watching the forklifts transporting pallets of smaller cargo to a storage area amidships. The big container loaders at the bow and stern were hoisting their tremendous burdens with ease under the watchful eye of a ship's officer, standing at one end of the bridge. Below him, two seamen were repainting the side of the hull with long-handled rollers, while further toward the stern two other crewmen were working on some lifeboat cables.

"You'll have to get aboard!" Dane insisted. He took her arm and firmly ushered her to the end of the steep gangway. "At this rate, they'll sail without us. I'll see you up in the lounge later."

Julie started up the metal incline, but she'd only taken a few steps when there was a warning shout from above. She froze, clutching the gangway railing as some metal object whizzed past her. It clanged noisily as it hit the edge of the railing close to her hand and then splashed into the water.

"What in the hell was that?" Dane called from the bottom of the gangway, his thin face working with shock.

"I . . . I . . . don't know. It all happened so fast." Her glance moved up then to search the decks of the freighter above her.

The painters were still painting, the men on the lifeboat were still crouched over the metal cable. Obviously, they weren't even aware of what happened. Her bewildered gaze moved to where the man had been standing on the deck by the Purser's Office, but his khaki-clad figure had disappeared. Julie looked back to where Dane still waited, staring up at her. She shook her head wordlessly.

He nodded, making a gesture that encompassed the busy dock. If there were any witnesses to the incident, they weren't rushing forward to offer their services. "Welcome to the *Anging Mamiri*," he said wryly, "and bon voyage."

"Thanks very much." She tried to match his manner. "You don't mind if I get under cover? I suggest you do the same thing. That wrench—or whatever it was—fell between us. It's hard to tell who they were aiming for."

He gave a disparaging shrug. "Just some ham-handed crewman probably, but that doesn't make it any better. I'll see you aboard."

Julie nodded and moved quickly on up the gangway to the safety of the covered decks. The sooner she got out of sight of that oily, mud-colored harbor water the better. She could only hope that what had happened wasn't an indication of things to come.

FOUR

After such an inauspicious beginning, the rest of her reception aboard the *Mamiri* was smooth and pleasant.

A young cabin attendant in a white coat was behind the counter in the miniscule Purser's Office and greeted her with a broad smile. "Mrs. Holdridge? Welcome aboard! I'm Lukie—your steward. Mr. Barnes, the purser, had to take some papers to the port officials or he'd be on duty. We had a health inspection of the steward's department this morning, so that made extra work." Lukie was taking a key from a cupboard on the wall as he spoke. "The purser will probably tell you about it at dinner tonight, since you'll be sitting at the same table with him and the chief officer. Now, if you're ready, I'll show you to your suite so you can get settled before we sail. Where's your luggage?"

"Coming. Mr. Hamill is still down on the dock taking care of it." An impulse made her ask, "Do your passengers have many accidents aboard?"

The steward shook his head. "We're not far from help on this part of the ship's run, and the purser's a pretty good medic at sea. Why? Were you worried about anything special?"

"Not really." Since she doubted if there'd be an epidemic of flying wrenches, she let the matter drop.

Lukie nodded, satisfied. "Of course, you'll have to wear flat heels if we hit any bad weather, but the chief steward will warn you about that."

"Fair enough." She was secretly amused by his brisk manner. The young steward was barely taller than she was, and he couldn't have weighed more than a hundred twenty-five pounds, but he had the assurance of a seasoned traveler. His skin was smooth and coffee-colored, a pleasing contrast to his wide smile and dark eyes. His black hair was straight, barely touching the collar of his white uniform coat. She guessed that he was in his late teens, but his faint accent was harder to pin down.

Julie made a diplomatic stab at it as she followed him up an inner stair to the deck above. "Is Okinawa your home port?"

"This place! Nuh-uh. I'm from Sumatra." Lukie led the way into a wider hallway on the higher deck. "Only one more week and I'll be on leave to see my mama." His dark eyes gleamed at the prospect as he held a door for Julie. "Down this way for your cabin. You and Mr. Holdridge have the suite on the port side. Mr. Hamill will be in the starboard one." He was leading her through an immaculate hallway where the waxed linoleum glistened under the overhead lights. "This is the passenger's laundry," Lukie paused to indicate a room with a modern washer and dryer plus an ironing board latched against the wall. Then he moved on to a cabin door and used his key. The metal door swung inward under his touch and he motioned Julie ahead of him.

She pulled up, delighted with the compact sitting room they'd entered. There were big square windows on two walls, with heavy oyster-colored draw drapes for nighttime or stormy weather. The same oyster shade was used for the wall-to-wall rug, and two small contemporary divans were upholstered in rust-colored leather. Oiled teak, banded with strips of brass, was used for the coffee and lamp tables.

Lukie proudly led her into the adjoining bedroom. The brass trim was picked up on the teak twin beds which were covered by beige bedspreads of a handwoven fabric. Two bureaus with brass drawer pulls lined one wall, and an impressive shortwave radio receiver was on a shelf above them.

The steward indicated a section of closets which would easily have stored enough clothing for a six-month cruise. Julie smiled as she thought of the sparse wardrobe she'd brought with her and walked across to inspect the bathroom with its tiled interior.

"You like?" Lukie asked proudly.

"I should say so. It's nicer than my apartment at home," she said, forgetting that she was supposed to be occupying Robert's elegant condominium. "Is the other suite as nice as this?"

"Almost the same," he told her. "That's why we never sail without passengers. I hear the waiting list is a long one."

"It all looks simply wonderful—I don't think I'll want to come out except for meals."

"Wait until you see the lounge. That isn't so bad either." He walked back into the sitting room of the suite and stared through the windows at the darkening sky. "You may have to spend more time in here than you'd planned, if the weather report holds. Sparks says that there's a storm coming up from the south and we're due to hit it later this afternoon."

"In that case, it's a good thing that the life jackets are handy on the closet shelf."

"Oh, you don't need to worry," Lukie said hastily. "There won't be any real danger. It's just uncomfortable because it's hard to walk around." He looked at his watch and started for the door. "I'd better see if Mr. Hamill has come aboard with the luggage. The purser will have my head if everybody isn't stowed away by sailing time."

"When *is* sailing time?"

Her question caught him partway into the hall. "The tugs will be alongside in a half hour," he said. "About enough time for you to get unpacked if I hurry." He let the metal stateroom door swing shut behind him.

A few minutes later she heard a knock on that same door and went to admit a burly crewman carrying her luggage. "Just giving Lukie a hand," he said. "Where do you want these, ma'am?"

"The bedroom will be fine, thanks." Julie tried to reach her purse for tip money but the man deposited the bags and was gone with a friendly wave before she could extract her wallet.

She started unpacking while the stateroom floor was still steady beneath her feet. Or at least relatively so, she amended, feeling the big freighter shift as two containers were settled into place on the bow below her stateroom window. She went to look and, fascinated, sat down on the divan to watch the ship being readied for sailing.

The final cargo adjustments were made just before two powerful-looking tugs came alongside to nudge the freighter out into the harbor channel. They maneuvered her past the end of the airport runway and around the breakwater, giving a farewell blast as the *Mamiri*'s bow cut into the gray waters of the Pacific.

Another knock at the stateroom door forced Julie to abandon her pleasant project of watching the spindrift sliding into the shallow valleys between the waves alongside the ship. She got up from the couch and went to answer it.

"Mrs. Holdridge?" A middle-aged man in his late thirties with brown hair and a mustache, wearing the khaki uniform of a ship's officer, towered over her. "I'm Jon Barnes—the purser. Sorry to be late in welcoming you aboard. Is everything okay?"

"Very much so." Julie stepped back. "Won't you come in."

"Thanks." Barnes hooked her metal stateroom door back to keep it open. "I suppose Lukie warned you about these doors. When there's any motion, they can be dangerous."

Julie was sure that he was obeying shipboard etiquette in keeping the door wide open, but she nodded and motioned him to a chair.

"I brought along a passenger information sheet," the purser said, handing it to her and then sitting down. "Mr. Holdridge supplied most all the data I need to know when he arranged for your tickets . . ." Barnes broke off to add, "It's too bad that he won't be able to come aboard until Singapore."

Julie murmured politely and dropped the passenger brochure on the table at her elbow.

"I'll have to collect your passport and health card whenever it's convenient." The purser put out a hand to stop her when she started to get up. "Just give them to Lukie some time in the next four days. I don't have to worry about my customers getting away from me." He checked his watch and then stood up himself. "We'll be dropping the pilot any minute now and I haven't finished my paper work. You and Mr. Hamill will be sitting with me and the chief officer at dinner, so we can answer your questions then. I'll send Lukie up with motion sickness pills if you think the weather's going to bother you."

"Don't bother, thanks. I've already taken one. Right now, jet lag is responsible for my gray look." She smiled at him ruefully. "When I'm seasick, I turn green."

The purser's answering grin made him look five years younger. "Just swallow those pills and use positive thinking. We'll keep you so busy on the *Mamiri* that you won't have time to be sick. Besides, our cook takes it as a personal offense if you miss one of his meals."

"I'll remember," she promised solemnly.

"The lounge on this deck is for passengers' use as well as the library and shuffleboard court on the deck above. Now I'd better be on my way. It's nice to have you with us, Mrs. Holdridge."

While Julie was still searching for a reply, he'd unhooked her cabin door and gone on his way.

She perched again on the arm of the divan, still basking in the warmth of his greeting. No wonder freighter passengers refused to change their lot. She glanced around at her luxurious surroundings and then sighed softly. Under other circumstances, it could be ideal. As it was, probably Robert would sleep on a davenport and she'd have the bedroom all to herself.

The pilot boat, edging carefully up to the *Mamiri*'s hull, distracted her from that depressing thought and she walked to the window to watch the transfer. As the freighter slackened speed, two crewmen went to the rail on the deck below, tending a collapsible metal ladder which had been let over the side. Even as she watched, one of the *Mamiri*'s navigation officers escorted a uniformed Japanese pilot, who was wearing white gloves, to the ladder where they exchanged salutes. The pilot climbed over the rail onto the ladder and, a few minutes later, had descended to the heaving deck of the smaller craft. He was assisted aboard by one of his sailors, and as soon as they were safely away from the rail, the little boat veered away and cut back through the heightening waves toward the breakwater. On the *Mamiri*, the crewmen stowed away the ladder and the powerful ship engines were accelerated to cruising speed. The outlines of Okinawa rapidly blurred in the thickening weather at the stern.

Julie didn't leave the cabin until she heard the chimes for lunch sounding in the corridor. By then, she had completed her unpacking, bathed, and changed clothes. Informality was stressed aboard the freighter, according to the publicity brochure, so she felt safe in a mulberry pants outfit with turtleneck top and hip-hugging sweater. Fortunately she'd brought along some canvas shoes to comply with the rule of flat heels and no-skid soles for rough seas.

Lukie was hovering in the hallway when she emerged, and looked relieved at her appearance. "I was afraid that maybe the motion was making you . . ." He waggled his hand suggestively.

Julie grinned back at him. "So far—so good. Ask me again later. That *was* the first call to lunch, wasn't it?"

"You bet. First and only," he advised, walking

ahead of her to show her the way. "The fastest route is through the lounge and passengers' bar."

She had to be satisfied with a quick look at a big lounge appointed with upholstered furniture, closed circuit television, and an elaborate short-wave receiver. Floor to ceiling curtains were pulled back from huge picture windows on two walls. At that moment the view from those windows showed acres of turbulent East China sea. Julie hastily averted her gaze and followed Lukie around the corner, past the small bar area which led directly to the officers' dining room. It was a cheerful place, with the half dozen tables covered with immaculate white cloths and view windows all along one side.

"Things are pretty informal at lunch time," Lukie said, pulling out a chair for her at a table for four near the door. "You and Mr. Hamill will sit here. The captain eats most of his meals in his quarters. If the weather stays like this, he'll probably be on the bridge most of the time. George here"—Lukie indicated an elderly black waiter who was walking surefootedly toward them—"will take care of you. I have to check on the laundry."

"Nice to meet you, Mrs. Holdridge," George said with a pleasant smile as he reached her side. He handed her a mimeographed menu. "Mr. Hamill sent his apologies. Says he'll see you at dinner."

Julie looked around at the empty tables. "You mean I'm your only customer for now?"

His smile broadened. "No, ma'am. There'll be some of the officers in a little later. Depends on their shift. Most of them sit over at that table against the wall."

Julie nodded and ran her glance down the menu.

"Just soup and dessert, please. I'm not very hungry."

George stared at her disapprovingly. "Have to eat," he warned, "even if you don't feel like it. An empty stomach's no good if it gets rougher, and the chief says it will be."

Julie was amused at everyone's preoccupation with digestion. Evidently nothing was sacred on the *Mamiri*. She only hoped that the captain wasn't going to receive reports on her physical condition as well as on the weather. "I feel fine, George," she assured him. "I don't have big lunches when I'm home, and they fed us all the way across the Pacific on the flight."

"Airplane food." George gave a disdainful sniff before he headed toward the pantry. "You'll like it better here."

He was back a few minutes later, bringing a half-full bowl of black bean soup and a basket of crackers. "Our cook's from New Orleans, so the menu runs mostly to red rice and gumbo on this trip. Let me know if you want something special."

"This looks delicious," Julie said, admiring the extra touch of a thin lemon slice floating on the steaming soup.

"I've saved a big piece of cherry pie for your dessert," George told her. "If you get hungry this afternoon, you can always go in the pantry and make yourself a sandwich." He picked up a pitcher of water and started pouring it over the starched white cloth on the table against the wall. "Gotta finish my damping-down before the others come."

"I thought you put up rails—is that what you call them?"

"Don't have rails on these tables," George told her. "Wetting the tablecloth does the same thing. Keeps the plates from sliding. The tables are chained to the floor—so are the chairs. Don't bend over to look," he instructed her sharply when she started to do just that. "Take my word for it. And don't try to save the dishes if they start sliding. Hang onto the table and let the china go."

She found herself obeying automatically as the *Mamiri* listed farther than usual, wallowing over a big wave. Just then the view from the dining room windows showed nine-tenths ocean and one-tenth sky. Julie clutched the edge of the table and saw George's wisdom in filling the soup bowl only half full.

The old waiter must have been watching her, because he put down his water pitcher and walked over to close the dining room curtains. "The reflection of that sun's too bright to be comfortable today," he announced, when he'd finished.

Julie smiled her thanks and went back to her soup. She knew that if she'd looked out onto that heaving sea much longer, she wouldn't have been around for dessert. She didn't hurry after that, enjoying the way the younger officers in their casual khaki uniforms came in and polished off tremendous lunches. There was little conversation and the slanting table tops did nothing to discourage their appetites.

When Julie had finished, she made her way carefully back through the deserted lounge. The curtains hadn't been pulled in there and one glimpse of the angry gray sea was enough to convince her that she didn't want to linger.

Lukie came out of the laundry room as she went

past on her way to the stateroom. "Lunch okay?" he asked.

"Fine, thanks." Julie kept one hand on the brass railing which ran the length of the corridor as the *Mamiri* lurched through a trough. "Doesn't this weather bother you?"

"Only if it gets worse," he said cheerfully, closing the heavy metal door and making sure it was latched. "The bridge gets the latest weather reports and the captain will detour if he thinks our course looks too dangerous. Don't worry—the *Mamiri*'s a tough one."

"I'll take your word for it." Julie felt a little foolish in her concern. "This is a good time to go in and take my nap."

"To get it over with," Lukie agreed, finishing the old joke. "I'm off duty now until dinner time, and I plan to do the same thing. Did you get all of your luggage that you needed?"

"Yes, thanks. I've finished unpacking."

He nodded approvingly. "Want me to take the cases and put them in dead storage with the others?"

Julie thought for a minute and then decided against it. Better not take any chances of getting her things mixed with Dane Hamill's in a storage locker. "There's no need. Not with all the closet space in my bedroom."

"Okay. I'll check again after Mr. Holdridge comes aboard." Lukie disappeared in the direction of the pantry, walking quickly despite the waxed corridor floor.

Julie went on the other way, giving a curious glance toward Dane Hamill's closed stateroom door before she let herself in to her own. She was surprised to learn that he wasn't a good sailor after all the traveling he'd experienced. Probably he'd done most of his trips by air and avoided the perils of seasickness. It was strange he'd chosen to come on the freighter at all; he looked far more like the expensive cruise ship type.

The fleeting vision of a green-faced Dane attempting a flirtation in the lounge, with the coffee table sliding back and forth in front of them on its length of chain, was enough to make her chuckle. So much for Robert's worries. If this weather kept up, the *Mamiri* would be as safe as a nunnery—and about as sociable, she decided, thinking of her solitary lunch.

When she awakened an hour before dinner, she was pleased to discover that her stomach had made peace with the ship's motion, and she was able to look out at the big gray waves through her cabin windows without swallowing nervously.

She changed into a simple shirtwaist in a cheerful brick shade and went to peer in the lounge. It was still deserted, but an attractive tray of canapes on the coffee table in the center of the room gave an indication of more sociable times to come. She decided to explore a little more and climbed a wide stairway to the next deck. There was a "Passengers' Recreation Area" sign atop a salt-encrusted window on some metal double doors. It showed a small shuffleboard court and stacks of aluminum lounges, which were roped against the railing. Julie decided it would be a fine place for sunbathing if the weather improved.

Another sign in the foyer indicated the "Passengers' Library." She went down another deserted corridor and came upon a book-lined cabin with big windows overlooking the bow. Lukie was in the process of drawing the drapes as she entered.

"I can leave them open if you want to stay up here a while," he said. "Just so the windows are covered when it's dark. This room is directly below the bridge and there can't be any light showing."

"Go ahead and draw them. It'll be dark soon and I'm just exploring before I go down to the lounge." She was inspecting the bookshelves behind grilled cabinet doors as she spoke. "There's a wonderful selection of books in here. Is it all right to take one?"

"Help yourself to as many as you like," Lukie advised. "The company furnishes most of them and passengers usually donate from their own collections."

"I'll remember," Julie said, selecting a mystery that she'd been wanting to read and tucking it under her arm.

When she returned to the lounge, Dane and the purser were sitting near the tray of cocktail snacks, glasses in hand. They got to their feet as she came in and Jon Barnes gestured her to the end of the couch beside him. "I was afraid you were going to give dinner a miss," he said. "It's nice to see both of our passengers up and around."

"Just barely," Dane said, sitting back down again on the other side of Julie. His face was a pale asparagus shade above his black turtleneck sweater. "I'm still not sure this ginger ale is a good idea," he said, indicating the glass in his hand, "but Jon says I have to start with something. God, wouldn't you know we'd hit the tail end of a typhoon!"

"Is that what it is?" Julie asked.

"Make it a 'tropical storm,'" the purser said,

passing her the canapes. "What can I get you to drink?"

A stricken look came over her face as she remembered some of the other instructions in the freighter pamphlet. "I didn't make arrangements to buy anything the way I was supposed to."

"As if that mattered," Barnes told her comfortably. "I had strict instructions from your husband to take care of your bar needs."

Julie was happy to learn that Robert had taken time for such details. Of course, there was nothing personal in it, she told herself before she got carried away with the idea. He'd made so many travel arrangements that it was simply second nature.

"Gin, bourbon, scotch, or does a Bloody Mary sound better?" The tall purser was waiting by the bar.

"Tonic water, please—with just a little gin," Julie told him as the *Mamiri* listed steeply.

Barnes nodded. "Not a bad idea—until you've found your sea legs for sure." He came back carrying a frosted glass and handed it to her. Then he sat down again and raised his own. "To the bride. I didn't know that you were a brand-new one until Mr. Hamill told me. I'll bet that husband of yours would like to be here now—despite the weather."

"Maybe it's just as well that Julie's on her own for the moment," Dane commented. "If she feels like I do, the honeymoon would go by the boards. A bed doesn't hold any attractions if you have to hang onto the edge of the mattress so you won't roll out."

The purser rubbed his mustache, trying to hide his amusement. "It might pose a problem. I'll tell

Lukie to stuff a couple life jackets under the edge of your mattress—that's what the rest of us do in rough weather so we don't bounce around."

"Is this storm going to keep on all night?" Julie asked, trying to disregard the way the lounge curtains were sliding back and forth on the rod as the freighter rolled.

Barnes grimaced. " 'Fraid so. We're skirting the edge of it. It's good that we aren't calling in at Taiwan this trip, or things would be worse." He took a long pull at his drink. "Both ashore and at sea."

Dane was studying the canape tray and finally chose an unadorned cube of cheese. "What do you mean by that? I hadn't heard of any trouble there."

"Not real trouble. 'Course the island authorities are always nervous since the Red Chinese started flexing their muscles on the mainland. We get a pretty stiff inspection every time we dock."

"Are they looking for contraband?" Julie wanted to know.

"That—and other things." Barnes swirled the ice cubes in his glass. "These days, the people on Taiwan aren't taking chances with anything. Lately, they've even had trouble with things going out of the country. I just saw a squib about it when I picked up an English paper in Okinawa," he went on. "Some of their choice art objects disappeared from the National Palace Museum. Incidentally, don't miss seeing the collection there if you ever visit Taipei," Barnes told Julie. "There are some absolutely priceless antiquities that Chaing Kai-shek brought with him years ago."

She nodded. "I'd better wait a while—imagine

what the airport customs are like these days if some of the national treasures are missing."

"There's no reason to suspect that whatever it was has left the island," Dane contributed, bending forward to search for another cube of cheese on the tray. "Exactly what are they looking for?"

"I think the newspaper account mentioned pieces of carved cinnabar lacquer from the Ming dynasty. They're almost priceless, but I guess they wouldn't be too hard to hide," the purser said thoughtfully. "These days, the museum itself sells plastic replicas of their choicer exhibits."

Dane whistled softly. "Well, it'll make a change for the Taiwan authoritites. Usually they concentrate on illegal aliens."

"I'm just glad they're not concentrating on the *Mamiri* cargo," Barnes acknowledged, grinning. "We're having trouble keeping on schedule this trip as it is. A customs search would really put us behind."

"They'll probably find the missing stuff still stored somewhere in the museum," Dane said. "I read the other day about a government official in Washington, D.C., who discovered a whole stack of valuable paintings in a basement annex."

A waiter came to the doorway of the lounge just then and sounded the chimes for dinner.

Dane took a resolute sip of his ginger ale. "The moment of truth—it had to come, I suppose."

"You'll be fine," Barnes assured him. He motioned for them to go ahead of him into the dining room. "The chief officer won't be down tonight. He sent his apologies and regrets. It's already gotten around on the grapevine that we have a pretty woman aboard, and if it weren't for this storm, he wouldn't be putting business ahead of pleasure."

A smiling George came to help Julie into her chair at the table as the ship rolled again. She was glad to see that the dining room's curtains were still firmly drawn, making it a cheerful ·haven from the stormy scene outside.

Unfortunately, the atmosphere wasn't enough to help Dane. He made a valiant effort to read the menu but the faint odor of onion soup which was being served at another table was too much for his queasy stomach. He shoved his chair back abruptly and stood up. "Sorry, I'll never make it. No—don't get up," he told Barnes. "Probably a good night's sleep is all I need. I'm sorry, Julie. See you in the morning."

"That's a shame," the purser said after Dane left. He looked up at George who was putting a basket of crackers on the table. "What do you think?"

"I'll have Lukie take some tea and crackers to him in a little while," the waiter assured them. "Five'll get you ten that Mr. Hamill will be in here sitting up and taking notice by breakfast or lunch at the latest."

"You're on," the purser said calmly.

"Okay. Do you want soup or fruit cup or both, Mrs. Holdridge?"

"Fruit cup, please," she responded, a little confused by the fast interchange.

George nodded and looked across at Barnes. "Both?"

"Both," he replied. "And roast beef for afterward. Don't let those vultures across the room take all the end cuts."

"I've got yours and Mrs. Holdridge's set aside,"

the older man said, and went to get their first course.

Barnes started buttering a piece of melba toast he'd selected. "I forgot to ask if this was your first trip to the Orient, Mrs. Holdridge."

"Julie, please," she corrected him, not daring to admit how her stomach muscles tightened every time someone addressed her by her new name. "I was in Hong Kong and Tokyo a few years ago but never down to Singapore or Indonesia."

"So that's why you chose this part of the world for your honeymoon."

Julie broke a saltine carefully and tried to think how a normal bride would answer. She could hardly say that Robert had the trip planned long before he thought of including her in it. "Actually, Mr. Holdridge—" She broke off as she saw the purser's eyebrows shoot up. "I mean Robert, of course. Since we work in the same office, I've gotten in the habit of . . ."

"Keeping things formal," Barnes finished for her. "I can understand that."

She let out a soft sigh, glad that somebody did. "Robert decided to combine business and pleasure on this trip. He's interested in early civilizations and wanted to explore the northern part of Sumatra. Afterward, we're meeting with some of the Indonesian tourist officials in Java."

The purser nodded. "I hope you'll be with us when we call at Bali later on. It's a gorgeous place, and there are plenty of ancient Hindu temples for your husband to visit."

"It sounds wonderful. But I don't know if we'll have time," she admitted wistfully.

"The home office has you booked for our whole cruise." He frowned as he saw her expression.

"Oh, lord! Am I letting a cat out of the bag? I'll bet that husband of yours planned to surprise you."

He looked so contrite that Julie intervened hastily. "Don't give it another thought. Robert will probably have to limit his vacation according to how business is going at home. Have you spent a lot of time in Southeast Asia?"

"Five years on this run." He waited for George to serve their first course and then picked up his spoon. "I spend most of my salary in Singapore buying jade and lacquer pieces. I'm crazy about the stuff." His expression was hard to define but Julie felt he was visualizing those attractive displays of *objets d' art* and wishing his salary would buy more.

"Maybe that's why you noticed the Taiwan museum thefts in the paper."

"You mean because I'm a frustrated collector? You're probably right." Barnes nodded as he thought about it. "People always zero in on the things that interest them. Take George—he's the sports expert on the ship, so he memorizes that section of the newspaper whenever we get in port. He knows the odds on everything from the Preakness to Wimbledon."

Julie finished the last bite of her fruit cup. "So I noticed. I suppose a lot of betting goes on aboard."

"It certainly does. The crew looks for any kind of diversion at sea. There'll be plenty of cash changing hands during the World Series, so it's just as well that Lukie's going ashore," Barnes added. "Otherwise he wouldn't have as much money to take home to his mother."

"You mean, he gets off at Singapore?"

"Singapore? No way." The purser grinned companionably. "Don't let him hear you say that. He'll have ten days off as soon as we dock at Belawan on northern Sumatra."

"He told me that he came from Sumatra." Julie's spoon stopped half-way to her lips. "Belawan sounds familiar, too."

"It's the port city for Medan," Barnes enlightened her. "That's where you and your husband go overland—across the island. We'll pick you up a little later, but Lukie doesn't rejoin the ship until we've been to Bali and Java."

"I should have been doing my homework," Julie confessed. "Things were a little confused before I left Los Angeles, and I barely remembered to pack a toothbrush."

"Don't apologize. If I ever get married, I'll be so unstrung that I'll probably leave my bride on the church steps."

Barnes broke off to watch George serve their two generous portions of roast beef. The waiter passed Julie a dish of sour cream for her baked potato and checked to see that they had everything they needed. "Coffee now?" he wanted to know.

"Later, please," Julie said.

"Same for me, thanks," the purser confirmed, and went back to talking about Sumatra. "Your husband requested that a car be available as soon as we dock in Belawan, but he didn't specify a driver. Do you know what he has in mind?"

"Not really." Which was an understatement if there ever was one, Julie thought ruefully. "You'll have to wait until Singapore and ask him then."

"Well, if it's possible, Lukie would like to hitch a ride with you. When I told him that you'd be driving through the Lake Toba region, you'd have thought he'd won on a sweepstakes ticket. The local bus transportation on Sumatra isn't exactly first class."

"You mean no schedules and complete with pigs and ducks?"

"Something like that. Since Lukie doesn't have much time off, he hates to waste a minute."

"That's understandable." Julie's knife slid off the edge of her plate and she retrieved it from the tablecloth. "Damn!"

"Don't worry about the laundry," Barnes reassured her. "Tablecloths come cheap. Broken dishes are harder on the budget."

"I'm not about to let this roast beef escape," she replied, smiling. "Getting back to Lukie—I'll certainly ask Robert. Even if he *has* arranged for another driver, there's no reason why Lukie can't come along."

"Maybe you'd better check first. After all, this is your honeymoon, and he might have made some special plans that don't include a third person."

"I'm sure he hasn't," Julie tried to sound brisk. "I won't promise Lukie, but you can tell him that the prospects are very good."

"Thanks, I'll do that. We'll be sorry to lose your company for that overland trip, but it's supposed to be fascinating country." Barnes reached for the horseradish and took another helping. "It wasn't too long ago that they practiced cannibalism in those parts."

Julie almost choked as she drew in her breath sharply. "You must be joking," she said when she was able to talk again. "I've never heard of such a thing."

"Word of honor." Barnes said, raising his right hand. Since he kept his fork gripped in it at the same time, it lightened the solemn pledge. So did the rapidity with which he renewed his attack on the roast beef. "Ask Lukie if you don't believe me. That Lake Toba area is the home of the Batak peoples, who have a history of cannibalism. There was a case just three years ago in one of their villages—something about a jealous husband who consulted a witch doctor and then followed his advice too enthusiastically. Naturally, the authorities hushed it up, but it was too late to help the wife. She'd been the main course for dinner the week before." The purser suddenly noted Julie's troubled features. "Sorry, I didn't mean to upset you."

She waved his apology aside. "I just didn't realize," she began and then interrupted herself to say incredulously, "surely the Indonesian government doesn't condone cannibalism in this day and age."

"Of course not. But the central part of Sumatra isn't exactly Fifth Avenue or Piccadilly. You're a long way from the fleshpots . . . Damn! There I go again."

"It's a good thing Dane isn't still around," she said, starting to laugh. "He'd really be under the table by now."

"You're right. Well, as I started to say—tribal authority still carries a lot of weight in the villages. You'll see what I mean when you get there."

"I refuse to worry about being eaten," she said with determination. "After what happened on the gangway today, I should be safe for the rest of the trip."

Barnes frowned across the table. "What do you mean by that?"

She felt a little foolish at having mentioned the

occurrence. "Just a 'near miss' when I came aboard. Somebody dropped a wrench of some kind and it whizzed past me. There was no use saying anything afterward—" Julie insisted when he started to interrupt. "All the excitement was over by then. Besides, nothing really happened—it just rattled Dane and me. He was at the other end of the gangway at the time."

"Maybe he's still getting a reaction."

Julie shook her head. "He's just feeling the motion. It's not surprising. The weather isn't getting any better, is it?"

"Unfortunately, no. It shouldn't get much worse if that's any consolation, but we'll be having a rough passage to Singapore."

"So much for life on the ocean waves," Julie sighed.

"The Pacific can be formidable at any month of the year, but October is one of the worst. At least you're still upright."

"With all this food being served three times a day, I intend to stay that way," she told him firmly. "I'll read in my stateroom the rest of the time." She hung on to the edge of the table as the freighter shuddered before righting itself again. "Now that I know the *Mamiri* isn't going to capsize every time it rolls, the prospect isn't so bad."

Barnes laughed with real amusement. "We're a long way from capsizing. If there's any danger of that, I'll come and take care of you personally. The chief officer and I have already reserved the lifeboat with a motor. The rest just have oars," he explained. "We'll let the captain take charge of those."

As the days passed, Julie became accustomed to the stormy seas. The weather remained ominous, with high winds which whipped the top of the waves to a froth and brought about violent rainstorms when the gusting dark clouds passed overhead. Lukie and George kept towels next to the outside doors to catch the puddles that seeped in.

Dane managed to appear at meals on some days, but it was a decided effort for him to be sociable. "My stomach has been going up and down for so long that I don't think it will ever get back to normal," he confessed to Julie at cocktail time the night before their arrival at Singapore. "It's a good thing I'm getting out of the travel business. I could never recommend a cruise to anybody after this bout."

Jon Barnes arrived, drink in hand, in time to catch the last of his remarks. "Don't let the captain hear you; he'd have you keelhauled." Then, passing a bowl of potato chips to Julie, he added, "I hope that you don't feel that way, too."

She shook her head. "I've gotten used to the motion, but I wish I could have stayed outside more. I planned to work on a suntan. Beating a steady track between the library and the dining room hasn't helped my vital statistics. I feel like that Shakespearean character who said, 'I am in the waist two yards about.'"

"That'll be the day," Dane scoffed. He took a sip of his drink and shook his head when Barnes offered the potato chips to him. "No, thanks. I notice that you haven't posted our arrival time in Singapore. Is that an oversight or deliberate?" As Barnes began to shake his head, Dane went on irritably, "Don't tell me there's been a change of plan on top of everything else."

Barnes sat up defensively. "Freighter schedules

are constantly changing. You should know that by now, Mr. Hamill."

Julie cut in to smooth the awkwardness. "We *do* arrive tomorrow afternoon, don't we? Otherwise I should let someone know."

" 'Someone' being your husband," Barnes replied, his annoyance evaporating. "You don't have to be concerned. He'll undoubtedly check with our representatives, and they'll give him the new arrival time."

"And what *is* the new arrival time?" Dane asked pointedly.

Barnes swirled the ice in his drink. "Nine o'clock tomorrow night. If things go as expected."

"But that's six hours late!" Dane protested, his drawn features tight with annoyance. "I hope you weren't planning any shopping, Julie."

She tried to shrug noncomittally. "We'll probably have some time in Singapore on the return trip, unless Robert has other ideas."

"He certainly has you well trained," Dane commented, not bothering to hide his anger. "Probably because you haven't been married very long."

Color surged under Julie's cheekbones at his accusation. Somehow he came perilously close to the truth every time he hazarded a guess. "This *is* a business trip for Robert," she managed to say calmly. "I came along at the last minute because he needed someone to take notes for him after he hurt his hand in a door recently."

The purser grinned in sympathy. "Any women I know would cheerfully close my head in a door if they thought they'd get a Far Eastern cruise out of it."

"What the psychologists would call motivation," she told him lightly.

"You don't have to worry on that score. I'm sure your husband didn't need any convincing to bring a bride along." Barnes winked at Hamill. "Otherwise, he would have found a secretary over here. Some of them can even take notes."

Julie rose as the dinner chimes sounded. "I'm too hungry to fight about Women's Liberation tonight. George told me that we're having roast beef again."

"Can't get a rise out of her," Barnes said, sounding sorrowful as he stood up. "And I was all set for a debate between the main course and dessert."

"I'd rather discuss our stay in Singapore," Dane said, walking with them to the dining area. "If we get in at nine o'clock, what time do we sail for Sumatra?" He pulled out his chair but waited for Barnes to seat Julie. "Early the next morning, I suppose."

The purser frowned. " 'Fraid not. The captain wants to make up for lost time. We'll be sailing again as soon as we refuel and pick up a few supplies. Mostly perishable items," he explained to Julie. "Fresh milk, fruits, and vegetables."

Dane cut into his explanation. "You mean that we'll sail by midnight?" he asked incredulously.

"I think so. Probably by eleven if everything goes smoothly, and in Singapore, it usually does."

Julie bit her lip as a new possibility occurred to her. "I hope that Robert's plane is on time. Otherwise, I won't know whether to get off in Singapore or stay aboard and meet him at the next port."

"Don't worry about it," the tall purser told her. "We're not about to leave you kicking your heels on an empty pier. I'm sure that your husband plans to meet our schedule or he would have sent a message by now. George would even bet on it."

"I should have thought to ask George in the first place."

"Of course." Barnes picked up his menu as the waiter started toward them, carrying a water pitcher. "Where do you think I got the information about our docking time?"

"Not from the captain?"

George arrived to overhear her remark. "Certainly not, Mrs. Holdridge. I got the news from the cook this afternoon..."

"And he heard it from the second wiper on the engine crew," the purser finished solemnly. "An unimpeachable source. He's the man who assured me that your husband will be waiting on the pier when we tie up."

"Which means you can put your money on it," George said, surveying them smugly. "I already have."

The lights of the tremendous Singapore harbor became visible the following evening at just past eight. The weather had softened and mellowed a few hours before. Julie leaned on the rail of the *Mamiri* as the big freighter threaded through the obstacle course of anchored ships in the famed port's outer reaches. The warning lights on the moored vessels formed a solid chain of color which eventually led to the magnificent "Lion City" itself.

The towering skyscrapers were outlined against the dark sky, as were the soaring hotel structures whose upper stories were often ringed in colorful neon. Overhead, there was a constant procession of jet-liners taking off from busy Payo Lebar International Airport at the outskirts of the city.

Julie was so busy looking at everything that she wasn't aware of the freighter's reduced speed until Jon Barnes's uniformed figure came up beside her.

"We're right on time picking up the pilot," he said in a tone of satisfaction, "so we should be tied up by nine easily. That means George will walk off with the betting pool again. It's a good thing he's a patsy for the American League, or he'd have gathered in all the currency on the ship by now."

"You sound bitter," Julie said, smiling.

"I am. I should have known better than to draw to an inside straight in the game last night," he admitted. "Are you excited at the prospect of seeing your husband again, or do modern women admit such a thing?"

"I think they do. At least, something's making my stomach muscles feel peculiar and I can't blame it on the rough seas any longer."

"I'll bet that he feels exactly the same way. It's too bad that he won't be on board long before you debark in Sumatra. We'll have to hold off any real celebrations until you rejoin us after the shore trip."

"I hope we can. Will Dane still be aboard?"

"Maybe." The purser lit a cigarette and dropped his lighter back in his shirt pocket. "Mr. Hamill isn't sure of his schedule either. He's paid for the entire cruise, but he said that he might have to cut the trip short." Barnes sounded thoughtful. "We don't usually carry such busy people."

"I didn't know that Dane was in the same boat. Sorry, no pun intended."

"I'll forgive you this time." The purser took a drag on his cigarette and exhaled slowly. "Mr. Hamill may be regretting his seagoing vacation."

"Oh, I'm sure that isn't it. He's starting a new kind of work and maybe he's apprehensive about it."

"What kind of work?"

She tried to remember. "Import-export, I think. It's funny that the subject hasn't come up."

Barnes started to laugh. "Considering the rotten weather we've had, Mr. Hamill was more concerned with the other things that were . . ."

Julie cut in as he hesitated significantly, "And you dared criticize my pun!"

"That's what a long sea voyage does to a man," he said, still laughing. "It won't be long before we tie up. That launch will be carrying immigration and port officials," he said, pointing at a small boat which was approaching. "After we satisfy the formalities, there'll just be time for a short social occasion."

"Which translates to 'drinks on the house.'"

"Exactly." He turned away and then paused to add, "Don't try to go ashore until the ship is cleared. I'll tell you when."

Julie nodded and watched him disappear around the corner of the shuffleboard deck. She reached for a head scarf as the breeze off the water grew stronger. It was a warm breeze though, and she remembered that the impending rainy season would make Singapore weather hot and sticky.

It was a wonder that she remembered anything, she decided ruefully as she stayed by the rail, watching the city's silhouette grow more distinct. The prospect of seeing Robert again tended to drive every other thought from her mind and raised havoc with her breathing. Even now, the first sight of the long quay where the tugs were nudging the *Mamlri* made her pulse rate bound.

Searchlights at the end of the pier illuminated a warehouse with a Marden steamship emblem and the words "Godown 14" on it. Julie decided to ask the purser what *godown* meant the next time she saw him. Then, as she tried to see the shadowed length of the pier, the lights along the side of the warehouse were turned on to reveal a crew of dock workers. There were men at the big bollards fore and aft of the ship ready to make the lines secure, plus others sitting in forklifts, and three uniformed men waiting for the gangway to be lowered. They were talking to two men carrying briefcases—probably local steamship representatives.

There was not a sign of the familiar figure Julie hoped to see. She stood frozen at the rail, unwilling to acknowledge the sudden despair that flooded through her. Could there have been a change of plans after all?

The magic of arrival seemed to fade; she became conscious of the fetid smell coming from the pilings below, and of the humid, almost oppressive, night air that was invading her clothes, making them cling uncomfortably. A water bird, disturbed by the docking procedures, soared over the wheelhouse with a mournful cry and disappeared beyond a West German freighter tied up at the adjoining pier.

Julie bit down hard on her lower lip to keep it from trembling, knowing that if she surrendered to her instincts, she would start making noises exactly like that unhappy bird. It was a good thing that Jon Barnes wasn't still around to see her making a fool of herself.

She stayed by the railing as the *Mamiri* was made fast. The gangway was being secured when she heard footsteps and turned to see Dane walking toward her. For the first time since they'd come aboard in Okinawa, he was dressed in a sport coat and tie.

"You look like a new person," Julie told him admiringly. "Did you get dressed to go ashore and arrange for an airplane ticket?"

He grinned and made a playful feint at her nose. "That's enough from you. The sight of land did wonders for me *and* my stomach." He looked down at the activity on the dock and said, "Hullo—I think we have company."

Startled, Julie followed his gaze and discovered that a taxi had drawn up by the end of the gangway to unload its passengers. Her heartbeat thudded when she recognized Robert's familiar figure. He was carrying an attaché case and had a raincoat tossed casually over one shoulder as he directed two ship's porters toward the luggage.

He had an awful lot of luggage, thought Julie, wondering whether he would ever look up at where she and Dane were standing.

Then her glance flashed back to that pile of luggage as she noted three of the pieces were shocking pink. Her eyes narrowed as she looked more carefully at the woman who was still standing by the taxi. She was breathtakingly lovely—a petite brunette dressed in black with crisp touches of white at the throat. Even as Julie stared, the woman moved over to where Robert stood and smiled up at him.

Dane gave a low whistle of astonishment.

"Where did Robert find her? And don't tell me she's an old friend of the family."

"I wasn't about to." Fiercely Julie hugged her arms across her breast, forgetting that she had felt stifled just a few minutes before. "I think I'll go down to the lounge."

Dane caught her arm as she started to move away. "Wait a minute. I'll see if I can get their attention."

"There's no need—"

"Of course there is." Dane put his fingers to his mouth and gave an ear-splitting whistle that penetrated even the noise and confusion on the pier.

Robert's head jerked upward and he waved as he discovered them. Then he bent his head, clearly urging the young woman to accompany him as he came to stand below them. "You're a little late," he called up. "We've been cooling our heels most of the day." He gave Dane a considering glance. "I didn't know you were aboard."

"I thought your wife needed company," Dane called back.

Julie opened her lips to deny it and then subsided when she saw Robert's measured, unwelcoming expression.

"Apparently I wasn't the only one," Dane was continuing, unperturbed. "Who's your friend, Rob?"

Robert's face lightened as he glanced down at the young woman clinging to his elbow. "Sorry—I forgot my manners. Mila, may I present my wife and Dane Hamill." Then he looked directly up at Julie and his voice carried clearly to her ears. "This is Mila Salim—and she's coming with us."

FIVE

There might have been natural phenomena which would have had a more drastic effect on Julie—like a typhoon in the middle of the Singapore harbor or a four-alarm fire on the dock—but for sheer, unadulterated shock value, Robert's announcement ranked high on the scale.

It also served to delay her greeting him. She had managed a noncommittal smile over the railing before turning to Dane and saying, "Excuse me, will you. I want to get something from my stateroom."

"Of course." He caught her arm long enough to say, "Where do you suppose Rob met her?"

"You'll have to ask him," Julie replied, keeping her tone determinedly cheerful. "Will I see you later in the lounge or are you going ashore when the ship's cleared?"

"Depends on the action." Dane sounded amused. "Why move to the suburbs if you don't have to?"

"Why, indeed?" In her present mood, she could have consigned him to the watery depths along with the man who, at that moment, was solicitously escorting Miss Salim aboard. "I'll probably see you later then." She walked over and opened the heavy metal door to go inside. Once it clanged shut behind her, she avoided the stairway leading down to the lounge and stateroom deck, making her way instead to the forward library. As she anticipated, it was deserted. She switched off the overhead light and then opened the floor-to-ceiling draperies. The window provided a fine view of the busy pier, but all Julie could see was Robert's face as he had introduced Mila Salim. Any romantic thoughts that she'd been cherishing since the afternoon they'd parted had abruptly sunk in the depths and disappeared without a trace.

Julie knew that Robert wouldn't flaunt his relationship with the Eurasian woman—she had enough confidence in his integrity for that. Mila was just an effective display to show that he hadn't changed his mind, that standing in front of a judge hadn't altered his future plans. Julie smoothed her forehead with tired fingers, aware that there wasn't much more time to hide. Dane would have said that she was en route to the stateroom, and if she didn't appear, everyone would wonder why.

For the first time, Julie felt the disadvantage, the physical limitations, of shipboard life. No matter how hard she tried, there was no escape for the moment.

Then she focused on the bookshelves by the end of the window and smiled cynically. She had a ready-made alibi right in front of her.

She walked over and pulled out a book at random, tucking it under her arm as she entered the corridor. The radio room opposite was securely locked and she encountered no one in the upper hallway as she made her way toward the stairs. At the bottom of them, she hesitated for a moment, debating whether to go to her stateroom or the lounge—and settled on the more public premises.

Dane and Mila Salim were laughing together over cups of coffee on the far side of the room.

They looked up in some surprise when Julie came to join them.

"I thought you'd gone to your stateroom," Dane said. "Or did you just come from there?"

She shook her head. "I got sidetracked picking out a book in the library and then I smelled coffee when I passed the pantry. Is George around or do we help ourselves?"

"There's a fresh pot on the burner in the bar. I'll get you some," Dane said, putting down his cup.

"Don't bother." Julie gave Mila a smile as she started around the corner. "Having coffee round the clock is one of the best things about freighter travel."

"If you feel well enough to drink it," Dane qualified. "I was telling Mila about the weather we hit on our way south." He hesitated and then came over to lean against the archway as Julie reached for a cup. "Did you know that Rob's looking for you?"

She looked up, wide-eyed. "Really . . ." and then broke off as she heard the lounge door open.

"I thought you said Julie was going to the stateroom," came Robert's irritable tones.

Dane straightened and peered out at him. "She got sidetracked. Don't worry, she hasn't jumped ship."

Julie took a deep breath and called calmly, "I'm in here, Robert. Would you like a cup of coffee?" She moved over to the archway and added, "It's good coffee—I can recommend it."

Her husband frowned and then belatedly remembered his role. He came over and cupped her chin with a possessive gesture, bending to kiss her. He didn't linger over it, but the kiss was hard, thorough, and without a trace of affection. "Where the devil have you been?" were his first words.

There was a pause while she tried to remember. Then it came back along with her resolve. "I stopped by the library." She picked up the book she'd brought and casually displayed it. "I didn't want this to disappear before I had a chance to finish it."

Robert reached over and took it from her, reading the title in a flat voice, *Elementary Blueprint Analysis for the Marine Engineer*.

There was another pause as she digested that. "Yes—well, it's surprisingly interesting."

"I'm glad."

"Would you like some coffee?" Julie said, trying for a safer topic.

"Okay." He waited until she'd poured it and went with her to join the other two by the windows. "Has the purser found a room for you?" he asked Mila.

"Yes, thanks. It'll be ready in about ten minutes." Her English was unaccented, as polished and urbane as her appearance. "Someone is going to give me the key as soon as the last official leaves. There's an officer's cabin next to the radio room that's vacant on this trip. That's the only reason they could squeeze me aboard." She gave Julie and Robert an arch look. "Don't feel that you have to stay and make conversation. I'm sure that you have a lot to say to each other."

"Yes, go ahead," Dane urged. "I promise to take care of Mila. We've already discovered a mutual acquaintance in Jakarta. Besides, I've had Julie on an exclusive basis for the past few days." His expression became even more pleased as he saw Robert's figure stiffen. "It's time that I shared the wealth. If you want a testimonial for our morals so far, you can ask Jon Barnes—he's the purser," Dane added helpfully.

"I know who Barnes is," Robert told him and then turned to Julie. "Do you want to take that coffee along to the stateroom?"

Since it gave her something to cling to, she nodded and followed him out of the lounge. She passed a lamp on the way and was sorry that it was fastened securely to the table. Otherwise she would have liked to detour by Dane and hit him over the head with it. Robert was still annoyed about her kissing Geoff Clarke; he'd never believe that Dane was making an empty boast about their closeness on the trip down.

As soon as the stateroom door closed behind them, her fear was borne out.

Robert put down his coffee cup and straightened to scowl at her. "I can tell that Dane hasn't changed since the last time I saw him. I only hope that you didn't fall for that 'rapture in the pasture' gambit of his. He tries it on every female he meets."

Julie stayed where she was, her back against the hall door. She was annoyed to find herself on the defensive when the situation should have been reversed. "I've never heard of anything so absurd," she snapped. "A tropical storm took splendid care of my virtue on the way here, if you must know. The only thing Dane was able to make on this trip was dinner—and that didn't happen very often."

"He wasn't suffering when I saw you up at the rail," Robert retorted, "and you weren't objecting to his pawing around then."

Julie's face showed her bewilderment, unable to fathom what he meant.

Robert made no attempt to explain. He strode over and stared through the window onto the pier below. "It doesn't matter—forget that I mentioned it." His voice sounded tired suddenly. "I'm sorry to hear you had a rough trip."

"It wasn't so bad." Julie was still smarting over his unjust accusation but tried to keep her own temper in check. "At least we didn't have to wait around the way you did. When did your flight arrive here?"

"Around noon. I thought I was cutting the connection too close until I checked with the Marden office and heard the *Mamiri* would be late."

"Did you meet Miss Salim at the steamship headquarters?" she asked casually, hoping to sound as if it didn't matter.

"Mila got in touch with me at the hotel when she found out that I was the other passenger joining the ship. I've known her for two or three years—ever since she was chosen as Miss Tourism by the Far Eastern travel authorities," he said, shattering Julie's last vestige of hope.

"I see," she said without expression.

Robert was equally matter-of-fact. "Beautiful woman, isn't she?"

Julie opted to tell the truth and go down with all flags flying. "Gorgeous . . . and she seems nice, too. Did you convince her to take the entire cruise?"

"We didn't talk about it." Robert glanced over his shoulder. "Why?"

If Julie had continued to be truthful, she would have said, "Because I'd like to know how long my competition's going to be aboard, that's why." Instead she retreated with pride still intact. "I just wondered," she said, moving over to put her coffee cup on a bureau inside the bedroom door. Lukie had been in earlier and stacked Robert's luggage at the foot of the nearest twin bed. "Would you like me to unpack for you? You shouldn't be using your hand any more than you have to." The words slipped out automatically. Then her eyes narrowed and she turned to look at his tall form more carefully. "What happened to the bandage? Now you'll just get those grazes infected when you're tramping around the landscape in Sumatra. Honestly, you should have your head examined."

Robert scowled back at her. "It's my hand and so far I haven't noticed any tendency for it to fall off. Besides, changing the bandage was a damn nuisance and I didn't have time to wait in line at a doctor's office in Paris."

Julie's own hand came up to her lips in an anxious gesture. "I forgot all about that air controller's strike. What happened over there?"

"They settled their differences the day I arrived. Unfortunately, there were a lot of our customers waiting for flights by that time, so it took a while to sort it all out. Then I flew back to the East Coast for a few days and finally came on here." He yawned mightily. "I'm not anxious to see the inside of another airplane for a while."

Julie surveyed him thoughtfully after he turned back to the window. He didn't sound like a man who was eagerly contemplating an energetic courtship. At that moment, he looked and sounded like somebody who would rather sleep the clock around—alone. She frowned and decided she'd better clear up that point right away.

Robert suddenly turned and pulled off his tie, walking over to toss it carelessly on the top of the bureau. "There's no need for us to hang around in here. I'd rather go outside with a gin and tonic and watch what's going on. Weren't there some lounges on that upper deck?"

Julie nodded but panicked inwardly. Just then, she had no desire to join the others and make lighthearted conversation until the *Mamiri* sailed. By morning, she might be better equipped to start playacting. "You go ahead. I can see all I want from the window here. Actually, I'm a little tired, so I'll make my bed on that divan." She gestured toward the one on the far wall of the suite's sitting room. "That way you can have the bedroom to yourself."

She braced herself for the inevitable argument. Robert would either insist on taking the divan himself or, worse still, reluctantly offer to share the bedroom. "I don't mind the inconvenience at all," she added aloud, forgetting that she was getting ahead of the script.

Robert's stolid gaze raked her slowly. "Okay. Do whatever you want. I'm going to change." He went over to his small suitcase and opened it, using his bruised hand somewhat awkwardly. He didn't have any difficulty, however, pulling out a sport shirt and pair of slacks.

Julie had the choice of unpacking his other bag or finding an avid interest in cargo loading. Neither seemed to fill the bill. "I'll take these empty coffee cups back to the pantry and get you another key to the liquor cabinet . . ." She broke off as

Robert muttered something. "I beg your pardon?"

He yanked off his belt and dropped it on the nearest bed before starting to unbutton his shirt. "Nothing. Don't worry about finding the liquor key. I have to talk to the purser before we sail anyway. Somebody called Lukie carried my bags up. He said there was something he wanted to ask me later on. Do you know anything about that?"

"A little." Julie pulled open the hall door and held it ajar with her hip as she picked up the cups. "He's our room steward and awfully nice. I think he'd like to hitch a ride in Sumatra with us. He has time off and will be going to visit his family there. It's right on our way."

Robert shrugged and pulled his shirttail free of his trousers. "Why not? The more the merrier."

Julie thought immediately of Mila and her own tone was as brittle as his. "Then that's settled. Incidentally, don't be concerned about waking me when you come in later."

"I won't." He had his shirt off by then and bundled it unceremoniously on top of his other belongings. "There's one other thing."

His last comment caught her halfway through the door. "Now what?" she asked crossly, having trouble keeping her gaze from his expanse of tanned chest.

"I plan to ask Lukie to bring early coffee around six," he announced.

"I don't see what that has to do with me," she began and then broke off to say incredulously, "You mean he'll bring it in *here*?"

Robert nodded and started for the bathroom.

Julie's voice rose in protest. "There's no reason

for me to get up at six o'clock in the morning just because you do."

"Nobody's asking you to." He pulled open the bathroom door, saying over his shoulder, "I'll tell him just to knock and leave the tray in the hallway."

"He can't do that. Nothing is left on the floor where it could slide around."

"All right then—you figure it out," Robert ordered coolly. "He could bring it in, but he'd see your bed on the divan and I'd prefer to keep the ship's gossip down to a minimum. Of course, you could always claim that you wanted to watch the sunrise."

"After a week aboard? That's absurd." Her tone was scathing. "It would be simpler if you went to the pantry and drank your morning coffee there."

"For you, maybe. Not for me." The words were pleasant but measured and firm. They also carried the undercurrent of authority often found in men accustomed to signing paychecks.

The latter fact was the clincher as far as Julie was concerned. Robert's marital authority was open to question, but there was no doubt about his status as her employer. There was also no doubt that he knew it. Her gaze dropped in defeat and without another word, she flounced into the hallway, letting the metal door thud shut behind her.

She deliberately killed time up on the flying bridge so that she wouldn't get back to the stateroom until Robert had gone on deck. She managed it successfully, evading Mila and Dane in addition when she skirted the lounge on her return. She was breathless as she closed the stateroom door behind her and leaned against it, aware of the suite's emptiness as she had never been before the ship reached Singapore.

Robert's open bag was still atop the bed. She moved slowly across the room and looked in the bath to see his toiletry case next to hers on the broad shelf below the mirror. Her fingers went out to touch the leather pouch and then she pulled them back, doubling them into a fist which she pressed hard against her lips. A moment later, she marched resolutely back into the other room and started stripping the blankets from her bed.

When she'd transferred them and a pillow to the sofa in the sitting room, she weakened and unpacked the carry-on suitcase Robert had left on his bed. It was a compromise measure, she told herself. The last thing she wanted when he returned to the stateroom was to have him stomping around half the night while she tried to sleep in the other room. It was going to be hard enough to pretend, since there was no door to close between them.

A glance at her watch sent her back into the bathroom to put on a pair of tailored blue pajamas whose only concession to femininity was a mandarin collar and monogrammed pocket. She slid her toes into satin scuffs and carried a thin matching robe when she came out into the bedroom. She switched on a table lamp to provide some illumination for Robert's return and then padded out to the sitting room. Once there, she yanked the curtains closed and put her robe on a chair before crawling under the blanket on the couch.

The shifting of containers at the bow provided a gentle rocking motion and she tried concentrating on that to get to sleep.

All at once, the cessation of motion in the ship's

Wait'll you taste Kent Golden Lights.

© Lorillard, U.S.A., 1978

100's only 10 mg. tar.

Kings only 8 mg. tar.

Taste 'em. You won't believe they're lower in tar than all the brands on the following page.

Kent Golden Lights: Kings Regular—8 mg. "tar," 0.6 mg. nicotine;
Kings Menthol—8 mg. "tar," 0.7 mg. nicotine av. per cigarette, FTC Report August 1977.
100's Regular and Menthol—10 mg. "tar," 0.9 mg. nicotine av. per cigarette by FTC Method.

Warning: The Surgeon General Has Determined
That Cigarette Smoking Is Dangerous to Your Health.

Compare your numbers to Kent Golden Lights.

100 mm Brands	MG. TAR	MG. NIC.	King Size Brands	MG. TAR	MG. NIC.
Kent Golden Lights 100's*	10	0.9	**Kent Golden Lights**	8	0.6
Kent Golden Lights 100's Men.*	10	0.9	**Kent Golden Lights Men.**	8	0.7
Benson & Hedges 100's Lights*	11	0.8	Kool Super Lights*	9	0.8
Vantage 100's*	11	0.9	Parliament	10	0.6
Benson & Hedges 100's			Vantage	11	0.7
Lights Menthol*	11	0.8	Vantage Menthol	11	0.8
Marlboro Lights 100's*	12	0.8	Salem Lights	11	0.8
Parliament 100's	12	0.7	Marlboro Lights	12	0.7
Salem Lights 100's*	12	0.9	Doral	12	0.8
Merit 100's*	12	0.9	Multifilter	12	0.8
Virginia Slims 100's	16	0.9	Winston Lights	12	0.9
Virginia Slims 100's Menthol	16	0.9	Belair*	13	1.0
Eve 100's	16	1.0	Marlboro Menthol	14	0.8
Tareyton 100's	16	1.2	Kool Milds	14	0.9
Marlboro 100's	17	1.0	Raleigh Lights	14	1.0
Silva Thins 100's	17	1.3	Viceroy Extra Milds	14	1.0
Benson & Hedges 100's	17	1.0	Viceroy	16	1.0
L & M 100's	17	1.1	Raleigh	16	1.1
Raleigh 100's	17	1.2	Tareyton	17	1.2
Chesterfield 100's	18	1.1	Marlboro	17	1.0
Viceroy 100's	18	1.3	Kool	17	1.3
Kool 100's	18	1.3	Lark	18	1.1
Belair 100's	18	1.3	Salem	18	1.2
Winston 100's Menthol	18	1.2	Pall Mall Filter	18	1.2
Salem 100's	18	1.3	Camel Filters	18	1.2
Lark 100's	18	1.1	L & M	18	1.1
Pall Mall 100's	19	1.4	Winston	19	1.2
Winston 100's	19	1.3			

*FTC Method   *FTC Method

Kent Golden Lights.
Full smoking satisfaction in a low tar.

Source of tar and nicotine disclosure above is FTC Report August 1977. **Of All Brands Sold:** Lowest tar: 0.5 mg. "tar," 0.05 mg. nicotine; **Kent Golden Lights: Kings Regular**—8 mg. "tar," 0.6 mg. nicotine; **Kings Menthol**—8 mg. "tar," 0.7 mg. nicotine av. per cigarette, FTC Report August 1977. **100's Regular and Menthol**—10 mg. "tar," 0.9 mg. nicotine av. per cigarette by FTC Method.

hull showed that the *Mamiri* was again ready to sail, and the familiar vibration of the propellers could soon be felt in the stateroom. Julie got up to peer around the edge of the draperies. The reflection of the lights on the pier confirmed there was a widening gap of water as tugs nudged the freighter out into the harbor again.

Julie cast an unhappy glance at the Singapore skyline, thinking how her mood of anticipation had been blasted on their arrival. Who would have dreamed then that she'd be skulking in the stateroom at sailing time while Robert was on deck with another woman?

She went back to the sofa and stretched out. Her blanket had come adrift, leaving her toes uncovered and icy but she determinedly ignored it, taking out her annoyance on the pillow instead. She thumped it soundly before she buried her nose in it and closed her eyes. This was the time to prove that she wouldn't be bothered by such minor inconveniences; she'd simply ignore them.

A half hour later, when all her vaunted attempts to relax had failed, she tried counting sheep. Only two fluffy lambs made it over the fence before she noticed that the second one bore Robert's rugged profile. Fortunately, she fell sound asleep before she discovered that the flirtatious bellwether ewe which was first over the bar had the name 'Mila' branded on its side.

SIX

The next thing Julie heard was a soft knocking nearby. When it was repeated after a discreet interval, she gave up thinking it would go away and sleepily opened her eyes.

It was a minute before she came to her full senses, and in that time she tried to focus on her surroundings. There was daylight at the edges of the drawn blinds in the sitting room, showing that her blanket had slithered onto the floor. Then her sheet slid down to join it when she shot a wild-eyed look at her watch and leaped out of bed.

It was Lukie in the hallway—bearing not gifts but coffee—and he'd be using his passkey to get in if she didn't do something fast.

She caught up her pillow and the blanket as she dashed over to the door. "Just a minute, please," she called breathlessly through it. "I . . . I . . . have to find a robe."

She didn't wait for a reply but swooped back to the davenport to get the rest of her bedding before plunging into the darkened bedroom. Robert was apparently still sound asleep, his motionless figure sprawled under the sheet on the far bed. The closest bed was stripped down to the mattress cover as a result of her actions the night before. She gave a despairing moan as her glance went over it. It was a dead giveaway if Lukie came in but there wasn't time for a salvage operation.

With efficiency born of desperation, she dumped the bedclothes she was carrying into the bottom of the closet and reached for her robe. Shoving her arms through the sleeves, she dashed back to the chair where she'd folded the bedspread and tossed it over the mattress cover so that it hid at least part of the glaring whiteness. Then, not daring to delay any longer, she ran back across the sitting room and unlocked the door.

"I'm sorry, Lukie." She was so out of breath that it was hard to get the words out. "I was sound asleep."

It would have been difficult to find a woman who looked less drowsy just then but Lukie kept a straight face. "That's okay, Mrs. Holdridge, I understand. Shall I put this tray in the bedroom?"

That triggered the possibility of Robert awakening, probably sitting up in bed to display his bare chest and shoulders. Julie wondered how she'd managed to notice that irrelevant detail in her frantic swing round the bedroom. She rubbed her forehead and tried desperately to think clearly.

Lukie didn't have much faith in her ability. "Is the bedroom okay or would you rather have it on the table in here?" he repeated.

"Here, please." Too late, Julie noticed her slippers by the edge of the divan where she'd kicked them off the night before. She tried to slide into them unobtrusively as Lukie bent over the coffee table to put down his tray.

At that exact moment, the bed light was switched on in the other room and there was a muffled expletive—just as if the occupant had looked at his watch and wondered what the hell was going on at that hour.

Lukie didn't keep him in doubt. He went

over to the bedroom archway. "Coffee, Mr. Holdridge," he announced cheerfully. "Let me know if there's anything else I can do," before he let himself out, closing the door firmly behind him.

Julie stood where she was for a moment. Then her simmering temper sent her into the bedroom just as Robert was reaching up to turn off the bed light. "You weren't thinking of going back to sleep, were you?" she asked ominously. "What about that early-morning coffee that you can't live without? Shall I bring it in here or would you rather have it in the other room?"

Robert rubbed his jaw and slowly pushed himself to a sitting position, yawning hugely in the process. He gave the distinct impression that the only thing he really wanted just then was to go back to sleep. After leveling a considering look at Julie, he evidently decided there was no hope for it. "In here, thanks. If you don't mind." The last words were a distinct afterthought.

"I don't mind at all—now that I'm up."

There was no more conversation until she brought the tray back, almost colliding with Robert by the closet. He was clad only in the bottoms of his pajamas. "Thought I'd better get a robe," he said, opening the closet door and stumbling when an untidy bundle hit him at the knees. "Dammit—what's all this!"

"My blankets and things." She scooped up the bed linen and deposited it on the end of her bed. "I had to do something with them in a hurry or Lukie would have been suspicious. As it is, he doesn't have any proof," she told Robert, who calmly put on a green foulard travel robe without bothering with his pajama top. "He might suspect that I didn't sleep here," she continued, feeling smug at the success of her earlier maneuver, "but that's all."

"I'm sure he doesn't have the slightest doubt as to where you spent the night."

"What do you mean?" Julie asked, not caring for the amusement in Robert's voice. "I didn't leave a thing out by the sofa except a pair of slippers."

"Who's talking about the sofa? Lukie just assumes that we both occupied my bed." Robert jerked his head toward the piece of furniture in question. "Perfectly normal assumption. You know—bride and groom, long-awaited reunion—"

"You don't have to spell it out," she snapped, angry because Lukie's idea of a honeymoon sounded like so much more fun. Before Robert could discover what she was thinking, she turned blindly to the tray and poured their coffee.

Robert knew that he was on shaky ground himself and wisely ignored her agitation. He sat down on the edge of his bed and yawned again. "It was late before we cleared the harbor. The chief steward and the purser rustled up a midnight snack and invited us to join them. I came in to see if you wanted a sandwich but you were sound asleep. I'm beginning to think you were the smart one." He yawned again. "I'd like to sleep for the rest of the week. Must be jet lag added to everything else."

Julie stayed by the bureau, drinking her coffee, but she sounded more like her normal self as she said, "Sleeping is the most popular occupation aboard."

"So I understand. Mila announced that she intends to spend her day in a deck chair." He was watching as he made that comment and didn't miss the way Julie's shoulders stiffened. "Does that appeal to you?"

"Very much." She crossed her fingers behind her robe. "I promised Dane that we'd take advantage of the first good weather." As she saw Robert's sudden stillness, she decided that the morning's skirmish was a draw. It was also time for a strategic withdrawal. She put down her coffee cup and pulled out a bureau drawer to get a pair of shorts and a sun halter, adding a wraparound skirt as an afterthought. "Do you mind if I use the bathroom first? I won't take long with my shower."

"Take all the time you want," Robert said, starting to take off his robe.

Julie paused on her way across the bathroom to watch him punch up his pillow. "Don't you feel well?" she asked, puzzled.

"I'm fine. Why?"

"For a minute I thought you were going back to bed."

"I *am* going back to bed." He suited his actions to his words, sliding between the sheets and stretching out with every evidence of enjoyment.

"But you ordered early-morning coffee. I thought you intended to get up."

His glance at the travel clock by his elbow was slow and deliberate. So was his shudder. "At this hour—not on your life. I'm going back to sleep for another couple hours. Don't let me change your plans, though."

Julie could have told him that her plans had included sleeping for two more hours, too, but that was before she'd been rudely awakened and drunk a cup of strong coffee. Now there wasn't a hope of going back to sleep again. She gave Robert's relaxed form a baleful look. For two cents, she'd throw something at him. Except if she tried that, she'd come out second-best again. Instead she had to content herself with muttering, "You'll probably miss breakfast. George likes to serve right on time."

"That's all right. Lukie said he'd rustle me up something from the pantry later on." Robert reached over for the bed lamp. "Mind if I turn this out while you're in the bathroom? When you're finished in there, turn it back on again if you like. I can sleep through anything."

Julie didn't get a vertical view of him until eleven o'clock that morning when he appeared on the shuffleboard deck looking fully rested and as if he'd just finished a satisfying breakfast. He surveyed his fellow passengers in their deck chairs and said mildly, "You all seem parboiled. How long have you been out in this sun?"

"It can't be too long for me," Julie informed him without moving.

Robert walked over and stared down at her, poking her thigh with an appraising finger. "I'd say you're past medium rare and not far from well done. Unless you want to be slathered in sunburn cream all the time we're in Sumatra, you'd better find some shade."

"I've been keeping track of the time," she protested. She didn't admit that she'd planned to move her chair into the shade earlier but had dozed off instead. "It might be easier if I stay aboard. Then you won't have to worry about dragging me along on that overland trip."

Dane raised his head in surprise. "I thought you were looking forward to seeing Sumatra."

"I'm just considering the possibilities," she started to explain.

Mila raised her sunglasses on her forehead and asked, "Who'll take notes for Robert then? It won't be easy to get another secretary at the last minute." She sat up on her lounge and smiled at him. "If I can be of help—just let me know."

"Thanks, Mila—I appreciate it," he said. "Let's see how things develop." He turned to Julie, letting his annoyance show. "I meant it when I said you should get out of the sun—" He broke off as the heavy companionway door opened behind him and Lukie poked his head out.

"I told Mr. Barnes that this is where you'd all be," the steward said triumphantly. "He wanted to invite you to a special cocktail party before lunch. Now that the weather has improved, the captain will be down to join you."

Mila got to her feet in a graceful gesture. "I love parties," she announced. "How formal do we have to be, Lukie?"

The young man surveyed her short shorts, string bra, and considerable expanse of smooth tanned skin. "Well, maybe a few more . . ." He searched for the right word.

". . . yards of material," Dane finished the sentence and got up himself, reaching for a shirt. "The same goes for me."

Lukie looked relieved. "Mr. Barnes said for you to come when you can. He's icing the martinis now."

"I'm glad I had time for breakfast first," Robert said with a grin when Lukie had disappeared back through the door. "It doesn't pay to oversleep on this ship. Coming, Julie?"

"In a few minutes. You go ahead." She was still

annoyed at his high-handed manner and didn't move from the deck chair, although the sun was beginning to feel like a soldering iron on her legs. "I'll meet you in the lounge."

His expression showed he'd like to argue, but all he said was a terse, "Well, at least get out of the sun."

"I will. As a matter of fact, I think I'll go up to the flying bridge for a few minutes. The view is wonderful and it's a good place to cool off."

"I wish I'd known about it," Mila said, as Dane helped her into a white cotton lace robe. "How do you get up there?"

"There are two stairs—on either side of this deck," Dane explained, urging her toward the door where Lukie had disappeared. "I'll show you after lunch if you like. That would be better than after the cocktail party."

"Why?"

"The stairs are steep and narrow—you need all your reflexes to negotiate them. Now, we'd better get changed or we'll keep the captain waiting. Are you coming, Robert?"

"I guess so." Robert looked as if he'd like to say more, but he turned and followed the others.

Julie waited until she heard the door close behind them and then quickly got up to seek shade under the roof of the shuffleboard court. A vision of their air-conditioned stateroom was even more appealing, but she decided to wait until Robert had left its confines before going down to change. After another moment or two, she walked over to take the forward stairs on the port side up to the flying bridge but discovered they were roped off because of fresh paint.

It didn't take her long to walk around to the

other side of the ship and climb the steep narrow stairs there. She made her way past the navigation bridge to the tiny deck alongside the freighter's big funnel. The railed platform was like a window to the world, with an unobstructed view to the horizon in each direction.

The sun blazed down on her, but its rays were tempered by the strong breeze which whipped her hair and cooled her sunburned skin. Far down below, the V-shaped bow waves looked like soapsuds atop the greenish-blue water. The big freighter moved steadily through the gentle swells, so different from the turbulent crests of the voyage south. Now there were soaring birds overhead and the bright membrane of flying fish to watch as they skittered atop the eddies next to the ship's hull.

Julie closed her eyes for a minute as she leaned on the railing, simply enjoying the peace and the solitude. Then she felt the heat of the sun on her shoulders even through the bite of the wind and knew she'd have to get in the shade or be in trouble as Robert had warned.

She was still thinking about him as she started back down the stairs, moving rapidly but keeping her fingers on the rail to steady herself. She'd passed the first flight and was three steps from the bottom of the second near the shuffleboard deck when she felt something come up against her right ankle. She staggered and tried to regain her balance, making a desperate grab for the other railing and missing it. After that, there was only time to see the deck coming up to meet her.

The jarring impact with the scorching metal made her gasp. She closed her eyes as an agony of pain forked through her left side all the way down to her foot. As she struggled to sit up a moment later, she saw blood oozing from her left shin. The sight made her close her eyes again and she bit her lip hard to fight off the dizziness brought on by the painful throbbing and the sun beating down. She couldn't faint—she had to get up, she told herself over and over.

She was mumbling the words when Robert came around the corner and found her sprawled in a dazed heap.

His exact response was lost in the blast of the noon whistle but he was still swearing steadily as he lifted her over to a shaded lounge by the shuffleboard court. Then he broke off to issue another order. "Just stay there until I get some help."

She caught at his trouser leg before he could move. "Don't go. I'm all right," she insisted as he turned back, his eyebrows drawn together in a forbidding line.

"You don't look it. Barnes knows first aid, and we're not far from help ashore if it's anything serious."

She moved her head back and forth on the padded chair cushion. "I tell you it isn't serious. I just banged my knee and shin. They hurt like the dickens, but I'll live."

He knelt by the side of the lounge. "Stop threshing around, will you. Are you sure you didn't hit your head? Or anything else?"

"I don't think so. I only missed the last steps." She grimaced and tried to steady her voice. "Now I know what 'hit the deck' really means."

Her feeble joke coaxed a slight smile from him. "Next time you try it, I'd recommend wearing a few more clothes." He got to his feet. "If you can hang onto me, we'll go down to the stateroom. After that, we'll discuss tactics."

"After that, I'll get cleaned up," she mimicked.

"I'm all for it. Right now, you look as if you'd been scraping barnacles." He kept his tone light to distract her as he bent down and helped her to her feet, keeping her shored firmly against his side. "We can avoid the crowd. Everybody's in the lounge enjoying the captain's liquor at the moment."

"It's too bad that you're losing out on the party," she said a few minutes later when they'd skirted the dining room entrance and reached the deserted stateroom corridor.

"I'll live. Besides, you're the one they're missing. Attractive women passengers rate higher on the social scale around here. If I hadn't come looking for you, the gold braid would have."

Julie waited for him to push open the stateroom door with his shoulder and help her through. "The way I look now, I wouldn't contribute much to the scenery."

"Soap and water will do wonders." Robert helped her to the nearest twin bed and swept back the spread with his free hand. "Lie down there. I'll get a wash cloth and start mopping up."

Reaction was setting in with a vengeance so Julie didn't argue. Resting against the pillows in the cool bedroom was so pleasant that she was surprised not to hear angel voices in the background. She was only half-aware when he returned with a thick bath towel and a basin of water. He sat down beside her and pulled off her sandals to bathe her injured leg. Afterward, her hands and arms were subjected to the same gentle but thorough treatment.

"That should pass muster," he finally reported in a satisfied tone. "It's a good thing that we don't have any walking on our itinerary in Sumatra. If you take it easy for the rest of today, you should be all right riding in a car after we dock tomorrow."

Julie brushed her hair back from her hot forehead, her troubled gaze following him as he went over to her bureau and started rummaging through the drawers.

"This should do the job," he said, after pulling out a sleeveless ivory satin sleep shirt and surveying it critically. "You don't want anything on that leg or on those sunburned shoulders either."

"Do you ever miss anything?"

He didn't bother to reply. Instead he came back to the bed and helped her sit up. "Raise your arms."

"But my halter . . ."

". . . will slip off under this," he said calmly, dropping the sleep shirt over her head. The halter was dealt with as efficiently; ties were unfastened as it was pulled away while the satin slid down.

With another deft motion, he pulled the sheet over her waist. "Now unfasten those shorts," he ordered.

"I can manage," she protested before he could do any more disrobing. She hastily squirmed out of them as he merely raised his eyebrows and left to put the towel back in the bathroom.

When he came back, he said, "If you're okay for a minute, I'll go explain what happened and make our excuses to the captain."

"There's no reason for you to miss the party."

"I'll survive," he said drily. "If I can find George or Lukie, I'll arrange for you to have lunch on a tray in here. You're not to put a foot out of that bed. Otherwise you won't feel up to the shore trip tomorrow."

"I *could* stay aboard," she repeated, mainly to hear his reaction.

"Unless you want more bruises, give up on that tack," he replied quite satisfactorily. "And don't try to dream up any more excuses because this time you're doing what you're told."

"We can discuss it later." Her declaration of independence lacked conviction because she really had no desire to be left aboard while he explored the mysteries of Sumatra by himself. Ever since he'd scooped her off the deck and brought her down to the cabin, he'd abandoned that bored, "couldn't care less" manner he'd exhibited in Singapore. She might still be a nuisance, but he was making it clear that she was *his* nuisance. That, at least, was a beginning.

In her dazed state it was easy to ignore all that had gone before. Especially her determination to avoid lying in the bed she was now occupying. She remembered her insistence on sleeping on the divan in the next room and wondered why she'd bothered.

"Julie . . ." Robert's voice cut into her musings and she lifted heavy eyelids to see him by the door.

"I thought you'd gone," she murmured.

"I was. I mean . . . now I'm back." He came over and sat down on the edge of her mattress. "Listen, Julie, you'll have to wake up long enough to eat some lunch. Then you can catch up on all the sleep you missed last night."

"And this morning," she added, not so muddled that she didn't remember Lukie's coffee delivery at dawn.

"I hoped you'd forgotten about that." Robert scratched the side of his nose ruefully. "We'll talk about it when you get your strength back. Right now, I want you to try and remember what happened just before you fell on the stairs. There wasn't anybody behind you, was there?"

She frowned as she thought about it. "No—there wasn't a soul around. At least on the stairs. I suppose there were people on the navigation bridge but—"

He cut in ruthlessly. "I'm just talking about the stairs. What caused the fall?"

"I don't know what it was—one minute everything was fine and the next—it was as if someone had grabbed my ankle and I was pitching forward." She frowned as she looked at him. "What are you getting at?"

"Just this." He chose his words carefully. "I noticed a length of broken twine on those stairs when I picked you up. I couldn't check it out then."

"But you went back?" Her voice could barely be heard.

He nodded. "A few minutes ago."

There was a pause which became even more awkward as it lengthened. Finally she could stand it no longer. "What did you find?"

"Not a damn thing. Either somebody decided to be all-fired neat and tidy or . . ."

"They decided to remove any incriminating evidence," she finished in a level tone. "If you don't at first succeed—try again. Did Dane tell you about what happened when we boarded in Okinawa?"

"I didn't ask him. The purser mentioned it

when I reported what happened today." Robert stood up. "It's probably just coincidence."

"If you're going to tell me fairy stories, you'll have to sound more convincing."

"Okay, so I don't believe it. At least you'll be okay in here for the rest of the day—providing you don't fall out of bed. And tomorrow, you'll only have to worry about Lukie's driving, tigers on the road, and the Batak witch doctors when we reach Lake Toba."

"I feel better already." She pulled the sheet up under her chin and tried to keep her voice casual. "Would you lock the door behind you when you go out."

"Why? What are you going to do?" he asked, scowling.

"Take two aspirin and write to my psychiatrist. There won't be time for it tomorrow."

SEVEN

Sumatra was hot. The stifling blast of humid air hit Julie as soon as she stepped outside the air-conditioned interior of the *Mamiri*.

Jon Barnes grinned at her from his post by the top of the gangplank. "Takes your breath away, doesn't it? You'll be glad to get back to us on the other side of the island. George is already putting up odds that you'll be early at the dock." His cheerful expression sobered as he saw the careful way she was walking. "Seriously—are you feeling up to the shore trip? The roads in northern Sumatra leave a lot to be desired."

"For lord's sake, don't mention anything else that can go wrong," Robert said, as he came up beside them.

"I was just making sure that you didn't take a plane back to Singapore from the middle of the island. I've been a little worried ever since I saw Lukie taking all that luggage off a while ago."

"It isn't all ours." Robert's tone was casual, so casual that Julie's eyes narrowed in suspicion. His next words showed that her premonition was justified. "Mila and Dane have decided to go with us."

"I'll be damned. They didn't say anything to me," Barnes exploded.

"They just decided. I met Dane in the corridor on the way down to get Julie. Apparently the home comforts of the *Mamiri* couldn't compare with the exotic lure of Indonesia. End of quote."

Julie wondered what else had been decided while Robert had left her to have his breakfast in the dining salon. "Is there going to be room in the car?" she asked, trying a feeble protest.

"No problem there," the purser assured her. "The Marden people have reserved a small van for you. Lukie has it out by the curb now—polishing all the chrome. He didn't expect to arrive home in such style." Barnes gave her another concerned look. "I hope you'll manage okay."

"I'm practically as good as new," she told him staunchly. "I don't know what was in those pills you sent along with lunch yesterday but I didn't surface properly until this morning."

Robert cut in, grinning, "Remind me to get the prescription. It's the thing I've needed for her all along." He turned at the sound of voices behind them. "Are you two ready to go?" he asked Mila and Dane as they approached the gangway.

"All set," Mila answered for the two of them. She was dressed in denim culottes and shirt with matching rope espadrilles which flattered her trim legs and ankles. Apparently the stifling heat didn't affect her at all. Dane wasn't so fortunate. His face was gleaming with perspiration and his short-sleeved sport shirt was clinging to his body just as Robert's was.

"I hear that you're deserting us," the purser said to them. "What made you change your mind about going overland?"

"Blame Dane," Mila replied. "One minute we were drinking coffee and watching Lukie take things down the gangway to store in the van and the next minute Dane announced that it would be a shame to miss the Lake Toba country."

"I still think it's a good idea," Dane cut in, "but I'd like to take the *Mamiri*'s air-conditioning system with us." He was mopping his forehead as he spoke.

"Don't begrudge us that. You're already making off with our choicest cargo," the purser said, indicating Mila and Julie. "Be sure that you bring them back to us at Sibolga."

"We'd better get going or we won't make Lake Toba by nightfall," Robert advised, "let alone the rest of the itinerary."

They made their way down the gangplank onto a dock crowded with curious onlookers. The friendly brown faces were all around them, falling back with smiles as Robert led the way past a two-story freight warehouse. It was marked with a Marden Steam insignia beneath lettering that proclaimed the Port of Belawan both in English and Indonesian.

Lukie was waiting beside a small van along with two uniformed port officials. The latter greeted them courteously, stamped their passports, and chalked their bags, which were in a row at the curb, without opening them. "Have a pleasant trip," the senior officer said in genial tones before nodding and walking off with his colleague.

"They're certainly casual," Julie said. "I thought the customs formalities here would be more thorough."

"I'm sure they've checked us out with the purser earlier. Some immigration officials came aboard with the pilot before the *Mamiri* entered the harbor," Robert explained. He turned to survey the pile of luggage on the pavement. "I'll help you load that stuff, Lukie. The rest of you can go ahead and get in. I wanted to be on the road before this."

Julie nodded, clambering up on the high seat of the minibus. She half expected Dane to help Robert with the bags, but he swung his camera case onto the back seat and followed Mila's trim figure into the van without speaking. He sighed as he sat down and mopped his face with his handkerchief again as they waited. "I hope there'll be some breeze when we finally get going," he said.

Mila gave him a puzzled look. "After all your years in this part of the world, I thought you'd be used to the climate. You look paler than poor Julie." She leaned forward then to ask, "How are all your bruises this morning?"

"Fine, thanks," Julie replied, wishing she could get off that subject before Robert returned. "I told Jon earlier that I'm practically in mint condition after sleeping all of yesterday . . ." She broke off as the rear door of the van slammed. Robert came forward to climb on the seat beside her while Lukie slid behind the wheel. "All set?" Julie asked.

"I think so. Finally." Robert folded his cotton jacket onto the seat beside them and bent to rummage in his camera bag on the floor. "What's first on the itinerary, Lukie?" he asked as the young Indonesian started the van and pulled away from the curb.

"We go first to Medan, which is about fifteen miles away," the other replied in a cheerful tone. "It's the capital of this part of Sumatra."

Julie had her own camera out as Lukie threaded the minibus carefully through the busy port area and finally turned onto a crowded two-lane road with people walking at its edge. She gave a gasp as the first car passed them. "I didn't know that you drove on the left-hand side in Indonesia."

"Even after we got our independence, we kept some of the Dutch customs, Mrs. Holdridge. That's one of them. Just the way they took some Indonesian ideas back to Holland. If you've visited Amsterdam, you're probably eaten *rijsttafel* dinners."

"And if you haven't, you can look forward to it tonight," Mila put in. "The hotel at Lake Toba has marvelous *saté*. I'm hungry already."

Julie nodded, but was too busy looking at the lush tropical foliage beyond the muddy shoulder of the road to concentrate on food. Evidently there had been recent rains and the sun was making the damp earth literally steam. *Becaks*, the bicycle-powered rickshaw conveyances, were everywhere. Most of the customers were native women, hiring them for shopping trips to the neighboring villages. Occasionally Lukie would encounter what he called *bemo opelet*, an ancient motorized vehicle used as a small bus. The passengers would be jammed in, but they all waved happily as Lukie tooled the minibus past.

It was when Julie commented on the attractive children walking along the roadside that Lukie said, "At least in this part, they have plenty to eat. Not like the big cities. In Jakarta, for example. Too many of the Javanese have moved there. Conditions are bad—very bad—when they try to make a living."

"How many Indonesian islands are there?" Julie asked him.

"Brace yourself," Dane cut in. "If George was around, he could win some money."

"I know there are quite a few more than the main tourist islands of Sumatra, Java, and Bali," she replied, trying to remember.

"That's a safe answer." Robert gave her a sideways grin. "Keep going. You haven't lost any money yet."

"Well, I read that there are three hundred main racial groups, two hundred distinct languages, and sixty percent of the population is under twenty-five years old," she went on, stalling for time.

"Very good," Robert approved.

"Much better than most visitors," Lukie concurred. "They're amazed to learn that we have over thirteen thousand islands—which makes for difficulty in our central government. Tradition is an important part of my peoples' lives and they resist change. That's why the old practices of the Batak—the people you are going to visit at Lake Toba—" he added for Julie's benefit, "continued until fairly recently. Now, of course, they live like the rest of us."

There was a moment of silence. Then Julie probed hesitantly, "By practices, you mean . . ."

"Cannibalism," Dane replied. "It was their way of life."

"But not now," Lukie said. "Now such things are outlawed."

"That didn't keep them out of the news two or three years ago when that village girl was sacrificed by her boyfriend," Dane told him.

"He and the witch doctor were later punished by the authorities," Mila put in. "Naturally the papers made a fuss over it, but there are equally horrible things in the headlines of other countries all the time."

"I didn't say there weren't," Dane replied. "I was merely telling what I'd read."

"Tomorrow we'll visit the Batak ancestral grounds at Samosir Island in the middle of Lake Toba," Lukie said to Julie, ignoring the altercation. "You can see for yourself what they're like. They have a style of architecture that's different from our other tribal groups."

"That's putting it mildly," Robert said. "The roof line of their house is patterned after the horns of a water buffalo. I think the main living quarters are supposed to represent the stomach." He sat back after putting his camera on the end of the seat within easy reach as the van passed a fairly deserted section of countryside. There were a few iron-roofed palm thatch huts on stilts at the roadside, but mainly there were simply coconut palms and papaya trees as far as the eye could see. "The houses here can't be compared with them," he concluded.

"There are a couple of sacrificial courts still in existence on Samosir, aren't there?" Dane wanted to know.

This time, Lukie's nod was reluctant. "They were preserved as examples of the culture, Mr. Hamill," he said, sounding defensive.

Dane uttered a short laugh. "Don't get upset about it. You can find beheading stones all over the world. Take Yucatan, for example. The Mayans have a real collection of sacrificial altars."

"And the French used a guillotine for the same kind of job," Robert put in drily, "so let's change the subject. It's too nice a day to dwell on horror stories." He turned to give Julie an appraising glance. "Feeling okay?"

She nodded and looked away from him to

concentrate on the scenery again. It was the only safe thing to do. Otherwise the color would wash up over her cheeks, showing that she was all too aware of his disturbing presence.

Evidently her maneuver wasn't successful just then because he said, "Sit over by me and rest your leg on the seat. There's plenty of room." He didn't give her a chance to argue, as he pulled her close beside him on the vinyl seat. "Now relax and lean against my shoulder. You might as well take advantage of any padding available. They haven't bothered with much of it in this van."

"You can say that again," Dane concurred. He propped himself against the door behind them as he tried for a comfortable position. "Where do we stop for lunch, Lukie?"

"There's a rest house about halfway to Lake Toba. It's run by the officials of a palm oil plantation." The steward braked and swerved around a man walking at the roadside, carrying a bamboo pole across his shoulders with Chinese-style baskets suspended from either end. "A cousin of mine works at the rest house, so there won't be any difficulties," Lukie continued a minute later. "We could have brought food from the ship, but I thought you'd enjoy eating Indonesian style."

"It sounds good to me," Mila said. "And the spicier the better." She bent forward to say to Robert, "Remember the *nasi rames* we had that time in Bali? The chef must have loved red pepper." She gave Julie a brilliant smile before going on to explain, "It's a mixed plate with rice and pickled vegetables. I hope that sort of thing agrees with you."

"I can hardly wait," Julie replied, hoping the fates would forgive her for such a whopping lie.

With the perspiration already gluing her clothes to her skin, the last thing that sounded appetizing was rice and pickled vegetables. She ignored the warning rumble of her stomach and stared through the van window again. At least the lush green scenery was restful, and there was always the hope that something else would be on the menu.

The next hours went by in pleasant, if uneventful, fashion. Once Lukie got through the outskirts of Medan, the bustling capital of the region, the traffic on the highway thinned to a mere trickle. But as the congestion lessened, so did the quality of the road, and before many miles passed, Julie was glad of Robert as a prop. Lukie did his best as a driver, but the narrow, winding pavement was studded with potholes and he often had to swerve off onto the shoulder when they met trucks or a crowded village bus.

The gently rolling countryside looked like a travel poster for the tropics, with plantation holdings everywhere. There were banana palms first, and later, as they traveled further inland, foreign-managed rubber plantations with rows of trees stretching endlessly on either side. Lukie called their attention to the newer palm oil groves, planted when synthetic rubber had first caused a collapse in the market.

There were occasional villages with dreary-looking thatched huts where most of the inhabitants were wisely staying out of the midday sun and the stifling heat. A few women could be seen talking and filling plastic buckets under the communal water faucet.

"I wonder sometimes what people did before they invented plastic," Julie murmured, after seeing a pile of buckets for sale at a tiny hut

where the only other merchandise was soda pop
and cigarettes.

"God knows," Robert answered, sounding
amused. "How about that fruit stand—there's some
local color!" He reached for Lukie's shoulder and
said, "Stop a minute, will you. I'd like a picture
of that."

"Sure thing, Mr. Holdridge." Lukie slammed
down on the brake pedal and pulled off the road
with a flourish that made his passengers hastily
grab for anything to hold onto. For Julie, it was
the front of Robert's shirt and she found herself
uncomfortably bent around his camera as he tried
to hang on and protect them both. At the same
time there were two thumps behind them as Mila
and Dane slid into the back of the seat.

Lukie looked fearfully back over his shoulder
when the van finally slithered in the dirt and came
to a halt. "Are you all okay?"

Dane pushed himself upright, wincing as he
moved his elbow. "We are—but you won't be if
you try anything like that again. What in the hell
happened?"

"The brakes grabbed, but it was my fault . . ."

"No, it wasn't. It was mine." Robert said, after
he'd extricated Julie from his lens cap and found
that she hadn't suffered any damage. "Next time
I'll be more careful in my back seat driving. Are
you all right, Mila?"

The dark-haired woman nodded carelessly. "I
will be if you bring me some of that fruit. Rambutans are a favorite of mine, and this is their
peak season."

"Fair enough." Robert had the van door halfway open when he turned back to Julie. "Would
you like some, too?"

She was staring at the fruit stand display, trying to see if anything was familiar. "I would—if I knew which one was a rambutan."

"Mila can explain," Robert said, getting out. "I'll be right back.

"Wait for me," Dane said, following him. "Lukie, go buy an assortment of the stuff. I like my pictures to have people in them."

"Photography isn't a hobby—it's an obsession!" Mila declared, watching them go. "Has Robert always been so keen on it?"

"I think so." Julie's reply was evasive as she hadn't realized that he owned a camera until that morning. "Is that big melon-like thing that Lukie's haggling over called a rambutan?"

Mila giggled. "Hardly. That's jackfruit. The little purple ones about the size of an orange are mangosteens and the red hairy ones are the rambutans."

"Whoever ate the first rambutan must have been starving," Julie said, surveying them. "They look ghastly."

"That's just the outer cover. When you peel it, the fruit inside is quite delicious. I'll show you," Mila said, smiling at Lukie as he brought a string bag bulging with his purchases back to the van. "Pass me one of the rambutans, will you? I want to show Mrs. Holdridge how tasty they are."

Lukie's grin flashed. "I'll peel it," he offered, choosing one about the size of a small plum and shucking off the outer covering in the same way he'd peel an orange. The inner fruit which he handed to Julie was innocuous-looking, but she nibbled at it warily.

Mila and Lukie both laughed at her expression

when she discovered how refreshing it turned out to be.

"The mangosteens are just as good," Mila said, selecting one from the bag and peeling the sturdy purple skin. The inside sections were structured like an orange except for their white coloring, lightly veined with pink.

When Julie took a sample, she found that it was equally sweet and delicate. "They're marvelous. I certainly wouldn't have guessed."

"Which just shows that you can't judge by appearance," Mila said, choosing a rambutan for herself and peeling it with her slender fingers. She watched Lukie walk over to join Robert and Dane, who were talking with the women and their youngsters at the fruit stand. From the grins on all sides, language wasn't proving a barrier. "Dane must be getting used to the temperature," Mila remarked idly. "That's the first time I've seen him smile since we left."

"He's been feeling rotten most of the time," Julie commented. "The storm north of Singapore made him seasick and now the heat's bothering him."

"So he just traded one set of problems for another. It's too bad—he can be amusing when he sets out to be. Of course, you know him better than I do," Mila said.

Julie didn't rise to the bait; she simply switched lures. "It was an amazing coincidence that you and Robert got together in Singapore."

"Wasn't it?" Mila sounded smug. "Robert's a dear. I couldn't believe it when he said he was married. He doesn't seem the type."

"He thought it was a good idea at the time. Probably I caught him in a weak moment."

"And he needed your help on this trip—with his injured hand." Mila finished her fruit and wiped her fingers daintily on a handkerchief. Her eyes narrowed as she stared out at Robert putting his camera away. "He's made a remarkable recovery."

"Yes, hasn't he?" Julie was saved from any more conversation when the men came back to the van, still laughing from their send-off by the fruit sellers.

Lukie waited until the other two had gotten in, securing the door carefully behind them, and then went around to take his place behind the wheel. "About an hour to the rest house where we'll have our lunch," he announced. His eyes met Julie's in the mirror. "I hope you'll enjoy that as much as you did the rambutan."

"So do I." She kept a safe six-inch buffer on the seat so that Robert had plenty of room to put away his camera gear. When he finished, she said brightly, "I plan to sit up and take notice for the rest of the way. Did you get some good pictures?"

A flicker of amusement passed over his features but his voice didn't show it. "Very nice, thanks. Toss one of those mangosteens over here, will you. I could use an appetizer before lunch."

As it turned out, the appetizer course was the best part of the meal. When Lukie finally turned off on a dirt path bordering the grounds of the palm oil plantation, the van's wheels sank into a series of mud holes caused by recent rains. They lurched painfully up to an aging one-story building with screened doors and windows. It was surrounded by thick plantings of shrubbery which looked as if they would overrun the place in another few years.

Lukie's cousin was an amiable young man who

led them into a shadowed room full of empty tables and chairs. "We are the only customers this late," Lukie told them. He was giving the big room a worried look, obviously wishing that it was cleaner and more inviting. "At least, there's plenty of rice and fish that he can warm up for us. Unless you'd rather have meat—" he broke off doubtfully.

A vision of fruit salad and a frosty glass of iced tea flashed briefly in front of Julie's tired eyes and then was banished resolutely. "Whatever's convenient will be fine," she murmured.

"I'll tell him," Lukie said. "In the meantime, there's beer that's pretty cold."

"Stop right there," Dane told him, pulling back two wooden chairs for the women and then settling down beside them. "Just start bringing the bottles and don't stop till I give a signal."

Unfortunately, the beer wasn't able to work miracles and there was no disguising the fact that the rest of lunch wasn't inspired. The prawns served with the rice weren't fresh and the chef had attempted to hide it by dousing them with a red pepper sauce. Julie choked and made a desperate grab for her beer after taking one bite. There was a side dish of peanuts and fried coconut which helped, but the other offering of shrimp puff crackers had succumbed to old age and humidity. Julie finally just moved the food around on her plate and wished she'd brought a sandwich from the *Mamiri* pantry.

Lukie was still apologizing for the meal's shortcomings when they got back in the van. "The food at the hotel by Lake Toba is very good. They'll even prepare western-style meals if you want them, but we'll be getting in pretty late tonight to ask for that," he added hesitantly.

He looked so anxious that Robert spoke up. "There's no reason for them to go to any trouble. I'm looking forward to a real *rijsttafel* dinner."

Julie knew that the *rijsttafel* consisted of twenty or more side dishes around a central offering of steamed rice, so she took heart and ignored the empty spaces in her midriff as she settled back to watch the scenery again. It was mainly a repetition of the morning except that there was occasionally a bigger town of several thousand inhabitants to interrupt the string of plantations. She saw shops housed in tin-roofed, one-story structures which were furnished in stark, primitive fashion. Bicycle repair shops abounded, along with tailoring or dressmaking establishments where the shopkeeper would be seated at an ancient treadle sewing machine, chatting with friends as he sewed. Sometimes the shops would be fronted with a concrete slab. This kept small children from playing in the dirt, but since the pavement wasn't angled for drainage, they gleefully sat in the morning's rain puddles instead.

"The rainy season starts this month," Lukie announced as he slowed so that Robert could take pictures. "We need the water for the land, but it means there are lots of insects. Fortunately Lake Toba is on much higher ground, so there aren't many mosquitos. You're all taking malaria pills, aren't you?"

When he was assured that they all were, he settled back to his driving again, for the narrow curving road required all of his attention.

As the pavement climbed, they passed the last rubber plantation, where workers could be seen at the tree trunks tapping the sticky white latex. The higher altitude revealed terraced ricefields with even green rows extending for miles around the hillsides. Farm families were working knee-deep in the muddy furrows, stooping most of the time in back-breaking labor.

"It would be bad enough standing in that mud," Mila commented, "even if you didn't have to worry about snakes." She saw Julie shudder and nodded in agreement. "That's the way I feel about it, but the farmers know that pythons and cobras will kill the mice and rats eating the rice."

"Sometimes you'll see good-sized monitor lizards in the fields doing the same thing," Lukie put in. "Notice that water buffalo are used for cultivating the soil." He gestured toward a pair close to the roadside harnessed with a crude wooden yoke. "They're prized possessions for the families with the land. Incidentally, we're entering Batak country now."

"Better not let Julie run around loose," Dane warned Robert after hearing the announcement. "With her talent for getting into trouble, she could end up as the main dish in a *rijsttafel*."

All of them could see Lukie stiffen angrily. Robert said in a low voice to Dane, "If you talk like that, you're the one who'll be in trouble. You've tangled with the authorities in Taiwan so long that it's become automatic."

"I just ruffled a few official feathers. Hell, that's par for the course there." Dane leaned against the side of the van and closed his eyes. "This heat's making me sleepy. Wake me up when we get to Lake Toba."

Julie was tempted to follow his example. Her bruised shin was aching and it was hard to not relax against Robert when the van swerved to avoid potholes in the road's surface.

If Robert was aware of her efforts to remain upright, he didn't let on. He lounged against the other side of the minibus, his eyes thoughtful slits against the glare of the afternoon sun.

The road continued to wind steadily upward for the next half hour until suddenly, rounding a sharp corner, the awesome perimeter of Lake Toba was spread out before them.

"Fifty-six miles long and fifteen hundred feet deep in most places," Lukie announced in the tone of a proud father as they all sat up and took notice. "The big island in the center that you can just see through the haze is Samosir—where we're going tomorrow."

"Where do we stay tonight?" Julie asked, trying to hide her weariness.

"Parapet. It's a small resort town about five miles north of here. Not long now. Just enough time for you to get settled in your rooms before dinner." He looked over his shoulder as a sudden thought struck him. "Mr. Barnes only made reservations for Mr. and Mrs. Holdridge, didn't he?"

Dane groaned. "Don't tell me there's a Rotary or Elks convention in the middle of Sumatra!"

"I wasn't thinking of that," Lukie replied stiffly. "We're so early in the season that all of the hotels aren't open."

"If worst comes to worst, we can have them put cots in Robert and Julie's room," Mila said, getting out her compact to check her makeup.

Dane grinned as he looked at Robert. "That's your cue. You're supposed to offer her your bed and doss down on the davenport in the lobby."

"Thanks for clueing me in," Robert replied

drily. "Why don't we wait until there's any trouble before we panic." He slanted a wicked glance toward Julie's quiet figure. "Besides, I promised my wife that I'd stick close. Who knows what kind of reception we'll get?"

Julie forgot about remaining silent. She drew in a sharp breath. "You don't mean those stories about the Bataks?"

Robert burst out laughing. "Lord, no. I'm talking about the kind of wild life we're apt to find in the room. Every time you open a window in this part of the world, something comes calling. If you go into the jungles around here, it's apt to be a tiger or orangutan. At least in Parapet, we can settle for mosquitos."

It was difficult for Julie to refrain from groaning. She ached in every bone, her stomach was a veritable chasm, and now it appeared that dinner was to be followed by a mosquito chaser. When combined with a bridegroom who was behaving like a native witch doctor on the prowl for a new victim—the honeymoon could double as a horror bill at the local movie.

Lukie stomped on the accelerator and the van shot down the winding hillside road toward the shores of Lake Toba. "Boy, I'm looking forward to this!" he announced enthusiastically.

Julie muttered something and Robert's eyebrows went up. "I beg your pardon," he drawled.

She glared at him. "I just said that I was looking forward to it, too."

He grinned then, for the benefit of the others, and patted her hand. "So am I, darling. We'll make it a night to remember!"

EIGHT

Their resort hotel at Parapet was located right on the lakeside. It was a two-story contemporary building of stucco with an eye-catching display of six-foot poinsettias along one side. Inside, the modest lobby contained two brown vinyl divans in front of a small reception desk and a dusty display counter which doubled as a gift shop at the far end of the room. The souvenir stock it contained was sparse; two piles of postcards and some plastic-wrapped straw hats with "Made in Taiwan" marked on the packages. There was one element which wasn't in short supply, however, and had all of them sniffing inquisitively as they lined up to register. It was Mila who voiced the conclusion first.

"Garlic!" she said. "Somebody must be boiling a barrel of it around here."

Julie closed her eyes as the combination of hot air and essence of garlic enveloped her like a shroud. "Where do you suppose it's coming from?"

"Downstairs," Lukie told her, as he leaned against the end of the reception desk. He was relaxed and beaming since learning there were two vacant rooms to accommodate Dane and Mila. "That's where the restaurant is. Don't you like garlic?"

"I don't mind a little," she said faintly.

"A little garlic is like being a little pregnant," Robert spoke up at her elbow. "There isn't such a thing."

"Garlic is extremely popular with Indonesian cooks—you'll find it in most dishes," Mila added. "Sort of like curry in India or Thailand." She turned to Lukie. "Who'll bring our bags in?"

"I'll take care of the luggage," he promised.

"You can use some help. I'll only need my overnight case." Robert turned to hand their room key to Julie and ask, "Do you want all your stuff?"

"No." She shook her head, trying to think. "Just the tweed carry-on and my tote bag. Will the rest be all right in the van?"

"You can rely on that," Lukie promised. "I'm going to spend the night with a cousin who lives on the outskirts of town and he has a garage where I can lock up our things."

Dane shoved his key in his pocket with more force than necessary. "Well, I'd rather not take any chances. Send both of those black bags down to my room. I'm going to have a shower and then find where they keep the cold beer in this place." He disappeared down the long central hallway with determined steps.

"I recommend that you follow the same course of action," Robert advised Julie. "Leave our hall door unlocked if you're heading for the shower. There are still a few arrangements I want to go over with Lukie about tomorrow's schedule." He glanced at Mila who was standing at the end of the reception desk. "Are you all set?"

She nodded and waggled her room key significantly. "I'll be fine. I want to use their telephone before I get cleaned up."

"It's on the desk just through there," Lukie told

her, indicating a small anteroom. He looked around for the reception clerk, but she had disappeared by then.

"Probably on her way to tell the chef he has some new customers," Robert commented.

"It doesn't matter," Mila assured them. "I'll wait until she comes back if I have any trouble getting through."

Robert's gaze was concerned as he watched Julie go down the hall toward their room. Then when he was satisfied that she was on the right course, he winked at Mila and gestured for Lukie to accompany him out to the van.

Julie double-checked the painted number on the door at the end of the corridor with the key Robert had given her before she walked hesitantly into the room. Her first glance was reassuring and she went on in, letting the door close behind her. It was a cheerful room, painted white, with big windows on one side. Twin beds with some sort of metallic gold bedspreads occupied most of the middle of the room. They were pushed close to each other, separated only by a small night table with a spindly brass lamp atop it. Two stiff armchairs were under the windows and a mirrored vanity of uninspired but conventional style was along the wall at the foot of the beds. Julie dropped her purse on the foot of the nearest one as she walked over to open a window. After a struggle, she was able to raise the sash on a part with an outside screen and she took a deep breath of the fresh air that flowed in. It was warm and humid but helped to dispel the stuffy atmosphere. Then she turned back and let her gaze go over the room. Two hooks were missing on the gold draw draperies, but otherwise the housekeeping department couldn't be faulted. She went over to peer in the bathroom and noticed that there were towels piled on the tiled counter. A test of both faucets revealed that hot should be translated as lukewarm but cold was certainly cold. Then she noted that the soap dish was empty and grimaced.

She'd have to go find some, she decided, since Sumatran hotel rooms didn't include telephones. "Damn and double damn!" she muttered distinctly. She retrieved the room key from the bureau before walking back into the corridor again to look for a maid or bellboy.

There wasn't anyone in sight, although she heard the sound of laughter floating up the stairwell from the kitchen. She tossed a mental coin to decide whether to go down there or try the reception desk and the latter won. Wearily she trudged down the corridor toward the lobby.

Mila's voice could be heard as she approached the reception desk and she hesitated, loathe to interrupt, but the woman's next words were so surprising that Julie put out a hand against the wall to steady herself.

"Of course I understand how important it is," Mila was saying angrily. "Why do you think I staged a meeting with the man in the first place? I tell you—I haven't left his side since." There was a brief pause in the conversation.

Julie guiltily looked over her shoulder to see if anyone was observing her unorthodox behavior, but the corridor loomed emptily behind her.

"Well, that's why I telephoned to report," Mila was going on. "If I'm going to make a move, it will have to be tonight. It was too difficult on the ship. With luck, I can get him alone at this place, but it won't be easy."

Julie's eyes widened incredulously as she heard that, but then Mila spoke rapidly again. "I'll have to hang up now. He'll be coming back in a minute. Wish me luck—I'll let you know straight away if . . ."

Julie didn't dare wait to hear more. All she needed then was to have Robert come back in the door and announce her presence. She slipped quickly down the hall to her room without looking back and managed to get the door unlocked before she heard footsteps coming up from the restaurant on the nearby stairs.

A diminutive bellboy appeared with three bottles of beer. "Mizz Hamill?" he asked her hopefully.

She shook her head. "Sorry."

"You didn't order beer?"

Julie was tempted to take what the gods and the help offered but she restrained herself. She'd need a clear head to discover what Mila was talking about. "No beer," she told the boy regretfully. "Do you have soap?"

"Soap?" the boy repeated, clearly unfamiliar with that English noun.

His dark eyes looked puzzled, but a uniformed chambermaid came hurrying up the steps just then and resolved the issue by stepping into the breach. "You want soap, miss?" At Julie's nod, she said, "I get. One minute, please."

It was closer to five before she returned and knocked on the door. When Julie opened it, she darted into the bathroom and proudly put a tiny guest bar on the tile counter like one bestowing a crown jewel. "Soap," she announced and waited for commendation.

Never had a sliver of Ivory received such homage, Julie decided, and made the only response possible. "Thank you very much," she said, handing over rupees solemnly.

The maid smiled and left quickly, before the other read the rate of exchange on Indonesian money and realized her mistake.

She needn't have worried. Overtipping was the farthest thing from Julie's mind just then. She replaced the room key on the vanity and stared at her reflection in the wavy glass mirror without even being aware of it.

What in the dickens did Mila have in mind concerning Robert that she was calling long distance to report on it? Probably a business deal regarding future tourism in the area. It was a big market and still largely untapped, she remembered from remarks that Robert had let drop. He was hoping to get official sanction on this trip for the firm to develop an island off the Java coast, installing resort facilities to rival Bali's beaches and charms. Now, it sounded as if Mila's employers had an eye to the same end. Although why she thought she could accomplish more by getting Robert alone . . .

A wave of warmth suddenly swept over Julie as she realized what a determined and beautiful woman could accomplish given the proper circumstances. Mila couldn't persuade Robert to withdraw Holdridge interests, but perhaps he'd yield and take on a partner firm. The brunette would see that it was worth his while, one way or another.

Julie felt a twinge of pain and discovered she was clenching her hands so tightly that her nails were cutting the soft skin of her palm. She bit her lip in disgust and turned to haul the small overnight case she'd brought with her onto the bed. If she had a shower and took time to think about things logically, she might possibly come up with the right answer.

She pawed through her belongings absently, selecting clean underthings and a dressing gown that was packed on top. Putting them over her arm, she slipped into a pair of scuffs and then caught up her small zippered cosmetic bag which contained her shower cap and other essentials.

There was an impatient thud on the hall door just as she was heading for the bathroom. She opened it an inch or two and moved out of the way as Robert came in, clutching a chrome wine bucket containing ice and a bottle of champagne.

"I thought you were transferring the luggage," Julie said faintly.

"That didn't take long." He walked over and hesitated for a minute before putting the bucket down on the vanity top.

Julie stared after him as she closed the hall door. "Compliments of the management or did you detour by the bar?"

"The champagne came from the purser's stock, but it's Indonesian ice. I thought you looked as if you could use something." He was testing the chill of the bottle with the back of his hand as he spoke. "The ice needs a chance to work. Go ahead and take your shower but don't take too long—I told Mila I'd come to her room in a half hour. She's got something she wants to discuss before dinner." When there was no response to his words, he turned to find Julie hanging onto the bathroom doorknob as if her life depended on it. "What in the devil's the matter?"

It was hard for Julie to even be coherent just

then—let alone make an intelligent reply. Obviously Mila had succeeded in setting up the meeting. The rest of her plan should go as smoothly. Suddenly Julie became aware that Robert was waiting for an answer.

"I beg your pardon?" she said, trying to catch up.

"I just asked if you were going to take a shower." He gave her a perplexed look, clearly convinced she was suffering from heat or a case of arrested mental development.

"I'm going." She started in to the bathroom and then came back to the doorway. "Why do you have to see Mila now? I thought we were meeting her at dinner."

Robert sat down in one of the chairs under the window, frowning as he felt its unyielding surface. "I don't see what dinner has to do with it. My god, I hope the bed is softer than this thing," he said, getting up again to find out. He glanced across the room, surprised to see her still in the doorway. "Look—if *you* don't want to take a shower, would you mind sharing the wealth? At this rate, I'll be lucky to get my hands washed before I have to leave."

"Don't worry," she remarked acidly. "You'll have plenty of time to prepare for your social engagement."

"What in blazes has gotten into you?"

"Not a thing. At least *I* don't make dates with Dane when you're around."

"Meaning that you did when I wasn't," Robert replied, ignoring grammar. "From the way the two of you were huddling at the rail when the ship docked in Singapore, I gathered your acquaintance had flowered. Frankly, I thought you had more sense." He whacked the thin pillow and then stretched out on the bed next to the window. "I hope you don't have any long-range plans that include him. Dane's got women in every port."

"At least, he doesn't have one at Parapet—unlike some men I could mention." She went in the bathroom and locked the door firmly behind her. Her last glimpse of Robert's face showed it was safer that way.

The tepid water of the shower helped cool her annoyance but didn't do anything to ease her concern about his appointment with Mila. She couldn't admit that she was upset because of what she'd overheard. Robert would laugh at her fears or, worse still, suspect that she was simply jealous of the other woman's appeal.

Julie got out of the tub and reached for one of the towels as she stood dripping on the mat. An honest-to-goodness wife wouldn't have to resort to subterfuge, she thought, frowning at her reflection in the mirror over the sink. The judge in Los Angeles had just decreed that she was a secretary with legal sleep-in privileges. And secretaries, no matter what stature, didn't tell their employers that they couldn't keep a date with the beautiful and willing Eurasian woman down the hall.

Julie started to hang the towel behind the door and then stood immobile as a sudden thought occurred to her. She couldn't order Robert not to meet Mila but she might accomplish it in another way. At least sharing the same marriage license gave her a right to patrol the preserves.

She stepped into her new pair of tap pants and absently put on the oyster satin camisole with slim ribbons at the shoulders. Pulling in the drawstring waist, she speculatively eyed her reflection. If she'd been planning a course in seduction, it would have been hard to find a garment better suited to the task. A bare whisper of lace constituted most of the bodice but she could make a pretense at modesty if she wore her dressing gown over it. Pulling on that ankle-length wrap of matching Tuscany-style lace did add something, but modesty wasn't the right name for it. Julie looked pleased as she surveyed her outfit—or rather the lack of it—and knew very well that it wasn't happenstance she'd brought it along. So far, all she'd been to Robert was a confounded nuisance who snarled and required bandaging at intervals. He'd seen her in cotton pajamas and a simple sleep shirt; now he might be tempted to look again.

She ran a comb through her hair, deciding that it didn't look bad considering the heat and humidity. The same factors made her settle for the barest dab of powder to take the shine off her nose and a brief touch of mascara. After applying lipstick, she blotted it carefully—just in case it might be subjected to wear and tear—and applied a light misting of Shalimar where the lace bodice was the sheerest. She wasted a half minute more practicing a sultry smile and then discarded the maneuver—Robert would simply think that the heat had addled her brains.

An instant later, Robert showed he was thinking of something else. His hand hit the bathroom door so hard that she jumped five inches. "Want your champagne?" he called out.

"In here?"

"Why not? Apparently you're planning to spend the night in there," came his unfeeling reply.

With that kind of beginning, even a Hollywood sex symbol would have had difficulty getting into her role. Julie took another look in the mirror for courage and then, with thudding heart, opened the bathroom door.

There was an ominous silence when Robert caught a glimpse of her, and he did nothing to break it in the moments that followed. His only visible reaction was a considering expression which washed swiftly over his features before he turned away.

Finally Julie couldn't stand it any longer. "I want to apologize," she murmured.

"So I see." He walked across to the vanity where the champagne was cooling and borrowed two glasses from a water pitcher nearby. "I'll pour these before I get cleaned up."

Julie would have thrown something at the back of his sleek dark brown head if there'd been anything within reach. She knew she looked sensational and also knew that Robert was well aware of it. Under the circumstances she had expected a far different reaction. Maybe not a fanfare of trumpets, but any other man certainly wouldn't be fiddling with the foil on a champagne bottle when his wife was standing in the middle of the bedroom wearing her dignity and very little else.

Robert took his time pouring the wine, making sure that the icy drops on the outside of the bottle didn't mar the top of the vanity while Julie tried to decide what she should do next.

The *femme fatale* role was proving more difficult than she'd anticipated. It was one thing to watch such maneuvers in an R-rated movie and quite another to put it to the test in reality. If Robert had responded the way he was supposed to, she thought angrily, none of this damned soul-searching would be necessary. And it wasn't that he didn't know what to do. According to rumors, he was well acquainted with the female form.

She heard him clearing his throat and discovered that he'd moved from the vanity over to where she was standing, offering her a champagne glass. "Are you feeling all right?" he asked when she hastily took it from him, spilling some of the contents.

"Of course I'm all right." She used both hands in holding onto the glass to disguise her nervousness and took a hasty swallow of wine.

Too hasty, as it turned out; the bubbles went down the wrong way and she choked.

Robert retrieved the glass before she could do any more damage. He put it on the bedside table and then offered his handkerchief to mop her streaming eyes when she pulled herself back together. She looked up finally and found him trying hard not to laugh. That was the last straw.

"Oh, please, will you just get . . . out of here!" She had to break off her ultimatum in the middle because of a lingering hiccup.

The amusement left his face, and for a moment, he looked as chagrined as she felt. "For god's sake . . ." he began awkwardly, "don't act like a damned fool."

"Why not? Right now, I feel like one and nothing you can say will change it." Julie sank down on the edge of the nearest bed and wrapped her arms over her breasts as the blast of the hotel's air conditioning made itself felt in the room.

He muttered something unprintable under his breath and sat down beside her, putting a hand on her arm. "You feel like an iceberg. Haven't you got a sweater or something. . . ?" He was looking around the room until he felt her start to shake on the bed beside him. "Julie, what's the matter?" His tone of concern changed when he saw that it wasn't grief causing her convulsion—it was laughter. "Now what?" he wanted to know, lifting her chin so that she'd have to look at him.

"A sweater!" She went off into another gurgle of laughter. "Can't you see it? On top of this . . ." Her gesture encompassed the froth of lace and satin she was wearing. When there was no response, she raised her eyes again and encountered Robert's brooding masculine gaze. Only this time there was no amusement in his glance; it seared as it went deliberately over the deep decolletage of her bodice, lingered on her creamy skin, and then came slowly back up to her parted lips.

As he watched the color flood her cheekbones, he said softly, "You don't need these trappings. I had a very good idea of your vital statistics long before this." His hand moved lightly up her arm, his thumb skimming the soft inner skin, so that she gave an involuntary tremor when it reached the sensitive hollow at the base of her throat. "I'll have to bring you a book on 'Ten Lessons in Seduction,' if you're going to wear outfits like this," he continued whimsically. "In the first place, you turn off the air conditioning. That's so you don't freeze before you even get started. Second, you never gulp champagne—because that causes trouble at the crucial moment." His arm was around her shoulders by then, his hand cupping the back of her head, letting her feel the strength of his fingers.

She tried to get her breathing under control. "What kind of trouble?"

"This kind." He bent to her abruptly, before she could finish the question, parting her lips with a hard kiss that demanded and then possessed in turn.

There was no chance for Julie to do anything but surrender to the seeking caresses of his hands and mouth after that. No time to feel nervous or embarrassed at her uninhibited response. This was where she'd wanted to be all along—clasped tight in Robert's arms with his lips moving on hers.

He must have shared her feeling, because there was no trace of his usual cynicism as he raised his head an instant later to mutter roughly, "Julie—sweet Julie—what a chase you've led me all these weeks." Then his lips blazed a trail downward on her delicate skin until he found what he was looking for. Julie shivered with delight at his touch and pulled his head even closer.

Afterward, she couldn't remember which of them first became aware of the disturbance in the hall. It was the determined rapping on their door which finally made them reluctantly pull apart.

"Goddammit—now what!" Robert said, getting up from the bed. His hand wasn't altogether steady as he ran it through his hair before he looked at his watch. "Where did the time go? I promised Mila that . . ." He broke off as the knocking started again. "Just a minute—I'm coming," he called irritably, stuffing his shirt into his belt.

His last comment brought Julie's head up and she stopped retieing a satin ribbon which Robert had dealt with earlier. "You promised Mila what?" she inquired, noting that her husband had reverted to his normal behavior awfully fast. The last few stolen minutes might never have happened from the way he sounded.

"That I'd see her before now." Illogically, he frowned down at Julie's quiet figure as he stood by the bed. Her robe was back in position but it wasn't the kind of outfit for receiving visitors. "If she's outside . . ."

"Why not invite her in?" Julie sensed his masculine embarrassment and decided to capitalize on it. "Maybe she'd like some champagne."

"That's not the point and you know it." Robert wanted to order her into the bathroom but was leery of trying it. He scowled and strode over to the door, yanking it open just as the knocking started again.

In the hallway, Dane lowered his hand abruptly. "So you *are* in there," he began before Robert could say anything. "Don't look at me like that. Mila's the one who sent me. When you didn't show, she thought something had happened to you."

"I don't know what she thought could happen in my own hotel room unless I slipped on the soap," Robert countered, still annoyed.

"A midget couldn't slip on my bar of soap," Dane responded.

"Well, then—what's the panic?" Robert stayed adamantly in the middle of the doorway, ignoring Dane's curious glances which strayed past him. "Tell Mila that I'll be along shortly."

His casual promise brought forth an unexpected response from the room behind him. Julie called out silkily, "Robert, dear, why don't you invite Dane in to have some champagne?"

A broad grin split Hamill's tanned face. "Yes, Robert, why don't you? I'll even bring my own glass. You go ahead and keep your appointment with Mila. Julie and I will hold down the fort here." He would have moved past the other man except that Robert remained stubbornly where he was, with one hand holding firmly onto the edge of the door.

"I think not." Robert didn't raise his voice but there was a quality about it that made Dane take an instinctive step back into the hallway. "Give Mila our regards and tell her that we'll buy her a drink before dinner. We'll buy you one, too." He eyed Dane laconically. "To make up for your disappointment."

The ominous look remained on his face as he closed the door and strode back into the bedroom. Julie was sitting in the chair under the window, apparently concentrating on the state of her cuticle. Without hesitating, Robert walked over to her and lifted her chin so that she had to meet his eyes. "Very clever," he said softly. "Either you've played the game before or you're a fast learner. Don't try issuing any more invitations in that negligee or you'll have a hard time sitting down for dinner. I don't think your grandfather would approve and I know damned well that I don't."

Julie realized she was lucky that he hadn't called her bluff when Dane was there, but his arrogance fed her fury. "Yet it's all right for you to go calling in Mila's room—and don't tell me she was waiting around for you in mukluks and a parka." A muscle at the corner of Robert's mouth twitched and made her flare even more angrily. "You think it's funny! Well, I don't." Julie swept up some clean clothes from her suitcase, lingering long enough to add, "From now on, I'll do what I like, when I like, and with who—"

"Whom."

She broke off stiffly. "I beg your pardon."

"Whom—not who. Wrong word," he said calmly, pouring some more champagne, and finishing it. Then he put his glass down and walked toward the bathroom, setting her out of the way like a bowling pin as he came alongside. "You can get dressed out here. That's another thing you'll have to learn. When there's only one bathroom, it's community property, and you had your share earlier. Dinner's served at seven." He looked at his watch again as he paused on the threshold. "That gives you exactly twenty minutes to get ready."

The bathroom door closed firmly behind him.

NINE

It was closer to a half hour later that he led her down the stairway at the end of their corridor to join Dane and Mila in the hotel's window-lined restaurant which overlooked the blue expanse of Lake Toba.

There were two parties of Indonesians at the back bar who had apparently been partying for some time, for they were shouting amiably at each other and dancing to the noisy output of three guitarists in a niche by the bar.

It was easier to talk when the musicians put down their instruments a minute later. At least Julie could hear the waitress asking if she wanted to see a menu or take the specialty of the house.

There was a moment of silence while she looked at the others for advice. Then Mila replied, "Well, I'm hungry—even if the rest of you aren't. My vote's for whatever's ready."

Robert watched Dane nod and his glance flickered over Julie before he confirmed, "The specialty will be fine. What would you like to drink, Mila?"

"Beer, please." She shot an annoyed glance at him and Julie. "At least I don't have to worry about mixing my drinks."

Dane started to chuckle and then thought better of it. "Beer for me, as well. What about you two?" he asked Robert.

"Make it four bottles of beer," the other said, handing the menu back to the waitress. "It's the best thing to go along with Indonesian food," he explained carelessly to Julie when the woman had disappeared through the swinging door to the kitchen. "They could do with a breeze in here," Robert added, reaching for a handkerchief to mop his forehead. "I wonder how the poor souls working in the kitchen stand the heat."

Dane jerked his head toward the group of customers at the bar who were still cavorting, even without music. "If you asked them, they'd say 'What heat?' I noticed that Lukie wasn't bothered on the drive down."

"Where *is* Lukie?" Julie asked, trying to ignore the temperature. Although she was dressed in a gauzy blue caftan and both men wore short-sleeved sport shirts, it was small defense against the soaring humidity in the room.

Mila was the only one who looked cool and comfortable in her white jeans and striped overshirt. "Eating with his cousin or nephew or somebody, I suppose," she said just then. "We can't really blame him—he doesn't have much chance to see his family."

"Well, as soon as he gets rid of us tomorrow on the other side of the lake, he'll be on vacation until the *Mamiri* makes her Indonesian loop," Robert said. "They pick up cargo in Java and Bali, so Lukie should have a decent holiday." He moved aside to let the waitress deposit iced bottles of beer in front of them and say that their dinner would be right along.

"Good. I'm starved, too." Robert reached for Julie's bottle of beer and automatically started to pour it for her.

"You don't have to bother," she told him stiffly, annoyed to find he seemed unaware that she'd been only coolly polite since he'd changed for dinner and reappeared in their bedroom. He'd simply picked up their key from the bureau, opened the hall door, and gestured her ahead of him. She'd had the feeling that if she hadn't been dressed and ready, he'd have left her standing in the middle of the room. So much for romantic interludes, she thought irritably, as she watched him under lowered lashes. Apparently his only regret was the fact that he'd had to disappoint Mila.

"No bother," he replied absently, keeping on with what he was doing.

"I don't even know if I'll drink it," Julie informed him, still sounding aloof. That was to let him know that she hadn't been consulted when the beer was ordered.

"You'll drink it," he assured her. "If this is a typical Indonesian meal, you'll need more than one bottle of beer to put out the fire."

Naturally he was right again. When the dishes were placed in front of them, family style, it was easy to see why soaring heat didn't bother the Sumatran people. Compared to the food, the temperature was insignificant. There was *saté ajam*—roasted chicken swimming in garlic-flavored sauce. Next to it was a dish of spicy vegetables called *sam balans*—also flavored with garlic, according to Mila. The steamed rice was happily left "*a capella*" but the tiny meatballs on a platter reeked of red pepper and garlic. Nor was the *sambal ati*, which turned out to be heart in red sauce, any better.

Between the garlic and the heat, Julie was forced to press the cold glass of beer against her flushed cheeks when she thought the others weren't looking.

Her action didn't go unnoticed. Robert leaned over to her when the guitarists in the corner started playing again. "You aren't eating very much. Too much spice for you?"

"I'm just not very hungry." She tried to sound convincing as she helped herself to another spoonful of steamed rice. Considering the amount of rice she'd eaten for lunch, they might as well be visiting China. She made a mental vow that if she ever did, she'd take along a package of instant mashed potatoes to break the monotony.

"Try the *seroendeng* . . ." Robert said, pushing a platter her way.

She surveyed it carefully. "I recognize the peanuts. Is that other stuff garlic?"

"You'll have to settle for coconut this time," Robert grinned, ladling it onto her plate. He was interrupted by the waitress coming over to whisper something in his ear and then gesturing toward the bar where a man waved jovially at him.

"Friend of yours?" Dane leaned across to ask.

"One of the government travel officials I met on my last trip. I'd better go over and say hello," Robert replied, getting to his feet. "The worst part is—he doesn't speak English very well."

"Then you can probably use me," Mila said, starting to push back her chair.

"Finish your dinner first," Robert urged.

"I'm going back to my room," Dane said. "Thank the lord, I don't have to worry about soothing official tempers any longer."

Robert frowned slightly. "It wouldn't hurt you to at least say hello. I'll buy you a drink."

"What about Julie?" Dane asked, not committing himself.

"Julie can go on to bed. We'll have another rough day tomorrow and she needs the rest."

"Any day now he's going to let me say a word or two for myself," Julie announced to the world in general. Privately she was thinking that the new development was another chance for Mila to get Robert by himself, which meant that she'd have to try again to prevent it. "I thought you wanted me to meet the Indonesian travel people," she said, detaining Robert by clutching at his shirt.

He stared at her in puzzled fashion and then calmly detached her fingers. "You'll meet most of them at the headquarters in Jakarta. There's no need for you to lose any sleep now."

"I don't mind at all. Besides, I won't be able to sleep until you come back to the room."

His eyes glinted with sudden suspicion but it didn't show in his voice. "Nonsense, darling—"

"It isn't nonsense at all," she said desperately.

"I won't be long." Robert's tone brooked no further discussion. "You go on to bed and get some sleep."

"What he suggests makes sense," Dane said, sounding the death knell. "Come on, I'll walk you to your room and we'll let these two work on business and diplomacy." He seemed to sense what was going through the other man's mind because he added, "Don't worry. It's too hot for me to get any extracurricular ideas in here, and there are too many mosquitos outside by the lake. Satisfied?"

Robert's eyebrows came together, but he didn't bother to answer the challenge. He simply gave Julie the room key and repeated that she shouldn't wait up. "I'll get another key at the desk when I come."

Dane deposited Julie outside the door of her room in circumspect fashion. "Robert's sense of humor seems to be wearing thin," he announced, handing back her key after unlocking the door. "I'm surprised that matrimonial bonds could work such a change."

"I like your choice of words," Julie said, amused despite herself. "A masterpiece of understatement."

"That's because I want to find my head still on my shoulders tomorrow morning." He bent to give her a chaste kiss on the brow. "Don't holler for help in the next hour or so unless it's an earthquake or a five-alarm fire."

"I'll remember." She hovered on the threshold. "Are you going back downstairs?"

"Nope. Robert doesn't need any help and Mila certainly wouldn't want me to hold her hand. Not now."

It wasn't the most reassuring thought he could have bequeathed. Julie frowned as she closed the door behind him and then, after a moment or two, twisted the knob and left it slightly ajar. That way she could tell if Mila tried to inveigle Robert down to her room. Although what could be done about it was a mind-boggling prospect.

Julie changed into a pair of tailored cotton pajamas which wouldn't raise anybody's blood pressure. As she put away the negligee she'd worn earlier in the bottom of her suitcase, she did her best to store her memories of that frustrating encounter, as well. Robert must have already put it out of his mind, or he wouldn't be holding an all-night business conference.

When Julie had finished brushing her teeth, he still hadn't returned. She cast a yearning glance toward the pillow on her bed even as she picked up a paperback and sat at the foot where she could hear voices in the corridor—thanks to the door which she'd left ajar.

It was hard to get comfortable on the rigid mattress and harder still to read under the dim overhead light. Like their European counterparts, Indonesian hotelkeepers believed any bulb over twenty-five watts was a clear waste of money. Julie leaned against the hard wooden footboard and sleepily turned another page of the book, trying to remember what paragraph she was on.

The next thing she knew, she was hearing a strange scratching noise and struggling to sit upright. When she managed, she realized that she was in bed with the sheet and bedspread neatly tucked around her. She sat up straighter in the gray light of dawn, trying to figure out how it had happened, when she heard the scratching noise repeated on the far side of the room.

Panicky, she checked the other bed and was relieved to see Robert's tall form stretched out beneath the sheet. Without thinking of the consequences, she got up and shook his shoulder. "Robert . . . wake up!"

He moved groggily and squinted up at her. "What's the matter?" Then he managed to focus on the travel clock by his pillow. "My god, it's only five-thirty!"

"I don't care what time it is. There's something in this room."

Robert frowned and pushed upright, showing a breadth of tanned shoulders and chest. "I don't see anything."

Julie gave the sheet bunched at his waist an uneasy glance, wondering if it was only the top of his pajamas he'd discarded. "I know," she hissed, "but I heard something. It sounded as if it was coming from my suitcase on that rack by the bureau. Listen, there it is again."

Robert nodded. "Stay here," he muttered and swung his legs out of bed. He hitched up the waistband of his blue pajama trousers, unknowingly settling Julie's mind on that score, and stepped in his slippers. "Is there anything to eat in that bag of yours?"

"Well, yes." She watched him walk soundlessly over to her open suitcase and peer into it. "Why?"

He reached for a tourist map on the top of the bureau and prodded at her belongings. "There he goes. Now let's see what he was after."

"There who goes?" she asked, deciding it couldn't be very dangerous or he wouldn't sound so casual.

"A mouse."

"Oh, no!" She made it to the top of her bed in one leap. "Where did he go?"

"Somewhere over by the window." Robert was pulling out a cellophane-wrapped bar from her suitcase. "He was having a snack on this fruit and nut thing."

"Damn! I was planning a snack on it myself today. Now I wish I'd eaten it last night," Julie said, watching Robert drop it in the wastebasket before he went over to their windowsill. "What are you looking at?"

"I was just admiring this lizard. He's enjoying the warmth in here." At Julie's sharp indrawn breath, Robert grinned over his shoulder. "Relax—he's harmless and only six inches long."

She collapsed onto her bed and shook her head helplessly. "That makes three kinds of livestock—there was a cockroach in the bathroom last night."

Robert walked back and got into his bed again, punching up his pillow before stretching out. "Your nocturnal habits probably confused him. I know they did me. Do you always read a book at the foot of the bed when the bed light and the pillow are at the other end?"

"Always. It's a habit of mine," she replied airily. "Was there another fruit bar in the suitcase?"

"I didn't notice."

If it hadn't been for the mouse, Julie would have gotten up to see for herself, but she debated the possibility of stepping on the wandering rodent against impending starvation and the mouse won. She sighed and put her head back on the pillow as Robert changed the subject.

"You must have left the door open last night, too."

"Did I?" Julie checked the clock on the bed table but decided it was hardly the hour to tell him of Mila's threats since hopefully he hadn't fallen victim to them. There would be plenty of chances to relate what she'd overheard later on. "I must be getting absentminded," she replied noncommittally. "Does it matter?"

"That's not the point," Robert argued, unable to ignore the intriguing silhouette of his wife's figure beneath the thin sheet. Suddenly he wondered why in the devil he was prosing on about unlocked doors when it would be safer to go back to sleep. He settled back on his own pillow, closing his eyes as he thought about it.

It was barely five minutes later when someone pounded on the hall door and shouted, "Good morning! Good morning! This is your wake-up call!"

Robert and Julie bounced up in their beds as if Vesuvius had suddenly erupted next door. "Dammit to hell!" Robert snarled. "What time did you tell them to call us?" The last was addressed to Julie's back as she started to collapse back into the pillow.

Injustice brought her upright again. "I didn't even leave a call," she said, pushing her hair back from her face and trying to think. "What time do we have to get up?"

"Not until seven-thirty."

"Well, then." She pulled the sheet back up to her shoulders and was already closing her eyes before she hit the pillow.

Robert muttered something profane about hotel management and followed her example. It seemed that he'd barely closed his eyes when the knocking was repeated.

"Good morning, good morning!" chirped the young voice again from the hallway. "This is your second wake-up call!"

That time, it brought groans from both their horizontal forms. Before they could make any other response, the alarm of the travel clock by their heads exploded with a shrill metallic buzzing.

"That does it!" Robert sat up to shut it off and then held his head. "This place makes an artillery range look sick."

"I'm sorry about the clock." Julie was examining it, her cheeks red with embarrassment. "I forgot that it's a little erratic." She noticed his resigned expression. "You look as if you had a hangover."

"I feel like it, too." He rubbed his jaw with the corner of his thumb. "Breakfast should help."

"I hope so. Do scrambled eggs in Sumatra come with garlic or without?"

A flicker of a smile went over his face as he got out of bed and felt for his slippers. "Play it safe and ask for boiled ones."

She watched him walk across to pull a robe from his open suitcase. "Are you going to get up? Officially?"

"Why not? I've heard of going against the tide but this is beyond me. If that guy yodels outside the door once more, I'll throttle him, so help me."

She started to giggle. "You should have a hook like they had on the old-time amateur nights—where the master-of-ceremonies waited in the wings and yanked off a contestant before the second chorus."

"If we were going to be here another night, I'd put it at the top of my list." Robert picked up his shaving kit and headed for the bathroom. "You might as well get some more sleep while I take a shower," he said, sounding like a husband of fifteen years standing.

Julie stared wide-eyed after him and then got out of bed herself. She knew very well that she couldn't match his nonchalance in their intimate surroundings so it was best to be dressed and ready before he emerged.

She was wearing an attractive tunic top and cotton skirt when he came out a little later. He was using a towel on the back of his hair, still damp from the shower. Before he reached his suitcase, Julie picked up her cosmetic bag and headed for the bathroom.

Robert bestowed a sardonic look as he stepped aside, showing that he was well aware of her tactics. "Nothing like a cool head in the morning," he commented. "But with those pajamas you had on, you needn't have worried."

"There's nothing wrong with those pajamas," she countered heatedly.

"Exactly. That's why you didn't have to worry."

There was no further discussion on the subject when they went down the stairs to the dining room a little later. The kitchen staff must have been roused by the same energetic bellboy as the guests, because the doors were open and the smell of coffee pervaded.

Robert sniffed the air appreciatively. "It makes a nice change," he said as he led the way to the table they'd occupied the night before. Dane and Mila were sitting at it, and looked up without enthusiasm as they pulled out their chairs.

"I take it that Paul Revere didn't miss your door this morning either," Dane said, making a token effort of getting to his feet and then collapsing again. "The only thing he forgot on his reveille roundup was a bugle."

Mila nodded an agreement, her lack of sleep evident by the drawn look of her olive skin and her lethargic glance. "It's too bad that tourist official isn't still around so we could lodge a complaint about this hotel. Between the mosquitos in my room and that bellboy, I don't think I closed my eyes for more than fifteen minutes."

Robert grinned as he scanned the brief menu. "At least we missed the mosquitos. I knew there was something to be thankful for." He turned to Julie, his expression suddenly serious. "Did you come through unscathed? I should have checked earlier."

"No mosquitos," she reported after an instant's pause. "All epidermis safe and accounted for."

Robert wasn't amused. "Are you sure? Even with antimalarial pills, there's always a chance of trouble."

"I'm sure. Believe me, I never ignore a mosquito no matter where it is." She saw the waitress approaching and was glad to change the subject. "Let's order. This is the only meal of the day that comes without rice and I don't want to miss a minute of it."

"You have plenty of time," Dane commented laconically after their order had been taken and the waitress had gone in search of coffee for them. "I can't see Lukie showing up early this morning. He certainly didn't waste any time taking the van and disappearing last night."

"I told him we'd meet him down at the pier for the lake steamer this morning at nine," Robert said. "He'll have our extra luggage aboard by the time we get there."

Dane waited impatiently for the waitress to finish pouring coffee all around before he asked, "Why does he need to bother with the extra luggage? We're coming back to the van after this damned boat ride, aren't we?"

Robert shook his head politely but definitely. "There's no point in coming all the way back here after we lunch on Samosir Island. Lukie will escort us to the mainland at the other side of the lake and let another driver take over there."

"You've lost me," Mila started to say when Dane waved her to silence.

"I wish you'd have announced your plans before this," he told Robert with some annoyance. "Now it's too late to do anything else."

"Not at all." Robert took a sip of coffee, grimaced, and reached for the sugar bowl. "You don't have to do anything you don't want to. Lukie knew Julie and I wanted to see the Batak way of life so he's arranged our itinerary accordingly. Naturally," Robert continued smoothly, "you and Mila are welcome to join us if you like."

Dane's ruddy complexion took on extra color as he was reminded of his guest status. "At this point," he said unpleasantly, "we don't have much choice. Frankly, I've had enough of this heat. I'd planned to find out about chartering a plane to the coast."

"It won't do you any good to get to Sibolga early," Mila reminded him. "The freighter won't arrive until later today, so you might as well stick around and suffer with the rest of us." She seemed to enjoy Dane's irritation and passed him a plate of cold toast which had just been put on the table.

"I didn't say I was headed back aboard the *Mamiri*," Dane countered smugly. "I was thinking more of a nice, cool beach in Bali."

Julie remained discreetly silent. She suspected that Dane would have quarreled with St. Peter at the heavenly gates just then, and she saw no point in giving him another adversary. Instead she concentrated on decapitating her egg shell with one stroke and almost succeeded. Since the egg turned out to be hard-boiled, it wasn't surprising.

Even so, breakfast tasted marvelous after her fasting of the day before.

She emitted a sigh of satisfaction when she'd finished a second piece of toast and marmalade. "I wonder if they'd mind if I took another one along for lunch," she asked Robert.

"I shouldn't think so, but that marmalade will get over everything."

"Not the toast," she protested. "I was talking about a hard-boiled egg. I could put it in my purse."

He grinned at her earnest tone. "Now you're beginning to sound like a real traveler. The first time I came home from Europe, the customs man in New York discovered some bread and cheese in my suitcase that I had left over from a train trip in Yugoslavia."

"*Now* you tell me," Julie countered in mock reproach. "That mouse last night was probably looking for your suitcase all the time."

"Mouse?" Mila's spoon stopped in midair. "What mouse? Where?"

"Not here," Robert put in quickly. "Forget it—family joke. I'll ask for a half-dozen eggs to take with us. We may all get hungry on the boat ride."

The eggs were duly delivered to their room after breakfast. Julie packed them carefully in her big shoulder bag after Robert offered to carry her camera to make up for the lost space. Breakfast had apparently improved his disposition, and even her mention of Dane's attitude didn't faze him.

"If he wants to charter a plane to get back to the bright lights—it's fine with me. I can't see why he bothered to come with us in the first place," Robert said, checking around the hotel room to make sure that they hadn't left anything behind. "Dane likes to be with a million people. He prefers beautiful unattached females, but quantity is the most important thing. That limits his selection here," Robert continued, still intent on the room's contents. "Dane isn't one to pursue a lost cause. Ready to go?"

She nodded and then said, "You've been wandering around for five minutes. Did you lose something in here?"

"You should know." Robert bent to pick up their bags. "Remind me not to recommend this place for any honeymoon tours."

She flushed under his gaze. "How would you know what would bother a real bridegroom?"

"There's nothing wrong with my imagination and I'd defy any man to survive the obstacle course in this place. Of course, a *real* bride," he continued, matching her tone, "wouldn't have a boy friend down the hall."

So he was jealous! Julie felt a glow of satisfaction that soothed her feminine pride, still tender from her abortive attempt to entice him the night before. "Now you're being ridiculous," she said.

"Oh, for god's sake, let's go!" He wrenched open the door, almost walking over the diminutive bellboy who was to carry their bags down to the hotel pier. Robert's disposition wasn't improved by Julie's choke of laughter as they sorted themselves out, and conversation was strictly limited until they joined Mila and Dane at the top of the beach stairs.

All thoughts of laughter left Julie when she sighted the tiny ferry which was to carry them across Lake Toba to Samosir Island.

The boat was barely thirty feet long and looked

as old as the Loch Ness monster. In fact, Julie decided after a second glance, the two of them had much in common. There wasn't a sleek line on the craft—the wooden parts were in need of paint and the canvas awnings had so many holes that there was a pattern of perforation. Two wooden benches on the after-section of the ferry comprised the passenger seating arrangements, since the bow space in front of the pilot house was already occupied with their luggage.

Lukie, wearing jeans and a deep-billed cap to shade his eyes from the bright sun, was waiting beside the plank which doubled as a gangway. "Everything's aboard," he announced with a cheerful grin as they came up to him. "Did you enjoy the hotel?"

"Fine, thanks." Robert said absently, making sure the hotel bellboy put their overnight bags with the rest of the luggage. Then he reached over to take Julie's elbow. "Might as well get aboard. Mila, you're next."

Julie bit her lip but made her way back to the stern as a solid-looking deckhand ambled toward the bow and the man in the pilot house managed to get the ferry's asthmatic engines going on the third attempt. She sat down hastily as the deck moved under her feet when the crewman leaned over to disengage the frayed bow line. "Is this the regular ferry?" she asked Lukie in an undertone while Dane and Mila were pulling their bench into the only available shade.

"It's the regular one on the off season," Lukie said. "Don't be worried by the way things look. There's never been an accident, and sometimes terrible weather comes up on the lake. You see,

Toba is big and deep—one of the largest and deepest inland lakes in the world."

His announcement wasn't the one Julie wanted to hear. "Where are the life preservers?" she asked after another survey of the wooden railing with two worn rope bumpers dangling from it.

Lukie stared at her and then followed her glance. "I don't know. They must be around someplace. I'll ask." He made his way forward, walking carefully because the ferry heeled precariously as it left the slip and set course for Samosir Island, which could barely be seen through the heat mist rising from the quiet water.

As they chugged laboriously along, Dane cast a disdainful glance over the side. "It's a good thing there isn't any weather," he commented. "There's practically no freeboard on this tub. With waves of any size, we'd be ankle-deep in no time. Maybe waist-deep."

"If you can't say something cheerful," Mila told him, "just look at the scenery. Besides, if worst came to worst, this bench should float."

Robert gave a snort from where he was braced against the wall of the pilot house, photographing the shore line. He looked around to see if there were any other picture possibilities and then replaced his camera in its case before coming back to sit beside Julie.

Lukie threaded his way back just behind him, carrying four bottles of pop. He sat down on the weathered deck between them to report. "The life preservers are down below with the engines, so there's no need to worry." He was fishing a bottle opener from his pocket as he spoke. "Refreshments are courtesy of the captain—to make up for the missing deck chairs. They've ordered new ones but they haven't arrived."

In the face of such hospitality, Julie decided it would be churlish not to match it. She accepted the cold drink with a smile and propped herself against the railing to enjoy the sun on her face as they cut through the smooth waters.

The lush greenery of the mountains surrounding the lake made a spectacular backdrop for Toba's expanse. Lukie's voice was full of pride as he explained how the lake originated from an early volcanic eruption and the area was later settled by the Batak people, currently comprising the largest protestant Christian population in all of Asia. "The majority of Indonesians are Islams," he concluded, getting up to collect their empty bottles. "About twenty million of them in all."

"How did the Bataks reconcile cannibalism with Christianity?" Dane persisted.

"I don't know, but those practices were followed many years ago," Lukie said, sounding affronted. "Today you'll see the beheading court at Samosir, but last night you could have attended a Batak choir practice at the church near the hotel. I imagine some of your ancestors did strange things too, Mr. Hamill."

"Some of my relatives still do," Robert echoed, ruefully. He grinned as he looked at Julie. "Talk about nuts on the family tree! They make your grandfather look great by comparison."

"He *is* great . . ."

"And I just agreed with you." His grin broadened. "Have a hardboiled egg."

Her own lips twitched. "No, thanks. Not yet." She pulled her sun hat down to shade her eyes and looked toward the approaching shoreline of Samosir. "Is that a village tucked in those palm trees?"

Lukie nodded. "A small one, but we'll go on to another place for lunch and then visit the local market. This first stop will show you remnants of that earlier Batak civilization I mentioned. There are some old houses in good condition and an ancient King's Court complete with beheading stone." The last was tacked on reluctantly.

Dane looked at Robert. "I can see your advertising brochures now, luring the tourists to the headhunters' paradise."

"I can't," Robert replied. "The architecture is the main attraction here, despite what you think. It's completely unique to this part of the world."

"Uh-huh—but that won't bring many customers." Dane's eyes were narrowed as he considered the wooden pier which jutted out into the water toward them. "It looks as if there are some small boats tied up there. Who do they belong to?" he asked Lukie.

"Local fishermen, I guess. There are a few families here who take care of the ruins. Why?"

"I was thinking of cutting my tour short. No offense, Lukie, but this isn't my bag—if you know what I mean." He gestured toward the bucolic village scene where they were going to tie up. Two children could be seen playing at the water's edge, but the only other sign of life was a large black pig rooting in the grass nearby. "I've been thinking I could hire a small boat and go back to Parapet now. There must be a charter plane there that I could hire to fly to the coast. We can all get together again later on," he added with a grimace at Julie and Mila. "It's not that I'm averse to your company—just this damn heat. Much more of it and I'll never make it to Bali."

"It takes getting used to," Lukie admitted. He hesitated a moment and then added, "I will make inquiries of the villagers if that's what you truly want."

Dane nodded. "Thanks, I'd appreciate it." He gestured apologetically to the others. "Sorry—I should have made up my mind earlier."

"No problem," Robert replied. "If you can't find transportation here, there'll probably be a boat for charter at our lunch stop." He was checking in his shirt pocket for extra film. "You should at least take a look at these houses before you go."

"I'll see. It all depends on what kind of a deal I can work out."

The stocky crewman left the pilot house and made his way to the bow as the engines sputtered off and the ferry's momentum carried them up to the side of the timbered pier.

"This place isn't exactly a hive of activity," Dane added, standing up when the craft bumped against the pilings and was secured.

"We're early for the season," Lukie said, getting up as well and extending a hand to Mila when the boat rocked in the shore currents.

"Don't apologize. It's better this way," Robert told him, steadying Julie with a grasp on her upper arm as they started to make their way forward along the narrow catwalk to the gangplank.

She peered idly down into the engine well as they came alongside and stopped to mutter something decidedly unladylike under her breath.

Robert's eyebrows went up and he grinned. "I didn't think you had that in your vocabulary."

"It's mild compared to what I'm thinking."

She pointed a finger down toward three inner tubes tossed in a corner beyond the engine. "*Those* are the life preservers on this thing. Three inner tubes for seven people."

Robert tried to think of something comforting and then gave up. "There's always that bench we were sitting on. Come on—let's get ashore. Maybe we can bring back a rubber duck."

Dane was waiting for them when they stepped onto the pier. "You'd better go on the tour while I do my negotiating," he said. "There's somebody down there on the beach with a fishing net, so maybe he owns a boat."

"I don't see anybody," Mila said, craning her head.

"Just beyond the pigpen. At least I think it's a pigpen," Dane replied, showing what he thought of the local architecture. "Although I don't know why they bother with a pen when they let that—creature—run loose." He was apprehensively eyeing the rotund black sow, who together with her three piglets was rooting noisily and sloppily in a mud puddle twenty feet away.

"Local color," Robert said calmly, focusing his camera. "They're not bothering anybody."

"Let's hope it stays that way. I'll see you later." Dane gave the pigs a wide berth and started walking along the narrow beach.

"This path goes to the *adat* house," Lukie said, leading the rest of them in single file up a dirt track which went past a tree-studded pasture where a water buffalo was stolidly feeding. The animal wasn't secured in any way but he exhibited no desire to join them as they filed past.

"What does *adat* mean?" Julie asked Robert

once the path widened and they could walk abreast again.

"It means the traditional way of doing things—the word comes from the Arabic." He pointed toward an exotic structure just visible through the palm grove over to the right. "Notice the shape of that thatch roof," he said, excitement in his voice. "Just like the shape of the horns on that water buffalo back there. Some of the newer houses have tin roofs—but that's the only change."

Lukie nodded. "You're right. There may be one of those in the compound but we'll see it a little later. Now come this way." He led them off to the left on a short path with a hedge at the end of it where he stooped and beckoned them to follow through a slight break and then stopped abruptly once they got past the barrier.

They were standing in a patch of grass before a waist-high circular stone perhaps three feet in diameter. Rimming it was a low stone wall enclosure, crumbling and darkened through age. "This is a sacrificial stone from the tribe's early history," Lukie began in an expressionless voice as he walked over and ran his hand along the edge. "To the Bataks, cannibalism was the way of life—they took flesh to gain strength and afterward burned the victim's bones outside the village so evil spirits wouldn't return." Lukie paused a minute. Then, when no one made an effort to break the silence, he continued, "Women and children of the tribe weren't chosen for the ceremonies—the Bataks made a practice of finding a strong enemy to use for their ritual. If the headsman didn't do his job well, then he was the next victim. The chief made sure of that. Unfortunately, the villagers didn't always wait for the sacrifice to die before they practiced their cannibalism. The more the victim screamed, the better . . ."

Julie cut in, hastily, "I'm sorry—but if I hear any more I'll be having nightmares. Why don't you go on with the explanation while I walk back to the ferry and get my sunglasses. In this glare, I really need them. It'll just take me a minute," she said, walking over to the break in the hedge before anyone could protest.

She didn't slow her steps until she was safely through and partway down the path. Then she stopped for a minute and took a deep breath. The stifling heat combined with Lukie's grisly commentary at the sacrificial stone had almost made her feel queasy. Even the sight of the bobbing ferry seemed welcome by contrast.

She narrowed her eyes thoughtfully as she saw Danc walking off the ferry at that moment with two bags in his hands. Evidently he'd found transportation back across the lake and was preparing for an immediate departure.

Just then, there were hurried steps behind her on the path and Lukie caught up, breathing heavily. "Your husband and Miss Salim have gone on up to photograph the houses. Mr. Holdridge was going to come and see if you were all right, but I told him I'd do it. I'm sorry that my explanation disturbed you," he added gravely.

She smiled. "Forget it. I'm not even happy watching horror movies on television. Besides, the sunglasses weren't an excuse—I really want them." She gestured toward Dane's figure on the pier. "Mr. Hamill looks as if he's about ready to leave us."

"But why is he taking your luggage?" Lukie asked, frowning.

Julie stared at the pier again and then glanced back at the young Indonesian. "I don't know what you mean."

"That blue bag he has beside him. The round one. It has your name on it," Lukie told her. "I remember very well. Mr. Hamill gave it to me to tag and store when you came aboard the *Mamiri* in Okinawa."

"He must have made a mistake," she began only to have Lukie shake his head.

"I remember it distinctly. He stayed around that day until it was done. I'll go and remind him now."

"No—wait!" She caught at his arm, not sure why she was doing it except that she didn't want an embarrassing confrontation between the two men. Dane was the type who would demand full retribution one way or another if he thought he'd been insulted. Not only the old Bataks wanted their pound of flesh, Julie decided even as she told Lukie, "I'll speak to Mr. Hamill about it. It's probably just a misunderstanding. You go on back with the others and I'll be along as soon as I get my sunglasses."

She walked rapidly down the path before Lukie could argue, and didn't look over her shoulder until she'd reached the pier. His slight form was disappearing behind the shrubbery hedge and she let out a sigh of relief. At least that was one problem less.

She walked carefully along the uneven planks toward the place on the dock where Dane had assembled his bags. He was checking the mooring line on a wooden fishing craft outfitted with an outboard motor, but he turned as he heard her approach. "Hi! What do you think of my transportation?" he asked.

She smiled at his dry tone. "Not bad—considering the place. The motor looks okay."

"That's what the fellow who owns it says."

"Where is he?"

"Around." Dane gestured vaguely. "I thought I'd be ready when he gets back. He has to round up the pigs or something. Maybe it was to tell his wife. We suffered a distinct communications gap."

"That wasn't the only one." Julie had moved over to his bags and was indicating a tag on the round blue one, an oversized leather tote bag with a locked zipper along the top. "This has my name on it. Lukie remembered that you said it was mine when we boarded the *Mamiri*. I've never seen it before."

Dane straightened slowly, letting the dinghy line fall at his feet. "What if I told you it was a present? That I was going to give it to you but I had second thoughts."

She stared back at him soberly. "I'd say that you should try for a better story."

"No, I mean it. It wasn't until afterward that I realized Robert might not approve. But by then, Lukie had put it in dead storage and it was too late. He wouldn't have understood either."

"I don't think I do." All Julie knew just then was that it might be a good idea to see exactly what Dane had put in the blue bag. She tried to keep her movement casual as she reached down and picked it up. "At least, give me a chance to see what I'm missing. Let's go aboard the ferry so we can have some shade . . ." she said over her shoulder as she walked back down the dock.

"No!" Dane's voice was sharp behind her. "Bring that back here. I'm warning you, Julie . . ."

"Warning me! What are you—" Her protest broke off and she started to run as he came toward her.

Before she'd covered six feet, Julie knew that she'd never reach the end of the pier ahead of him, and an instant later, she felt his rough clamp on her shoulder. He pulled her around with one hand and tried to drag the bag from her with the other. "Why the hell couldn't you stay out of it," he ground out as they struggled. "Now I'll have to take you along." His fingers tightened cruelly on her skin. "At least part of the way."

Another instant and he would have torn the bag from her grasp. But just then a piercing squeal came from the pig on the shore to shatter the still air. Dane's grip weakened long enough for Julie to yank at the bag and get away from him, ripping her blouse in the process.

A frantic glance around showed there was only one way for her to escape. Without hesitation, she took a step off the side of the pier and, still clutching the heavy leather bag, plunged into the murky cold water.

Despite popular belief, all the highpoints of her life did not flash through her mind as she plummeted down through the black depths. Instead she was wishing that she'd remembered to take a deep breath before she'd jumped into the water. Or even a shallow one. That was uppermost in her thoughts, along with a belated resolve not to panic on the downward journey. She wasn't a strong swimmer but eventually she'd bob back to the surface again and then she'd be safely out of Dane's reach.

She dwelled for quite a while on that thought. Dwelled so long that when she didn't have any breath left, it was too late to do anything about it. She did try to kick but there was no upward motion despite her feeble efforts.

The darkness of her surroundings moved in and invaded her mind before she had a chance to panic. There was an emptiness about her—a dulling lethargy. She even took time to remember Lukie's words about the Batak victims—"the more they screamed, the better"—before she- opened her mouth to do just that.

When she could think again, she was on the surface.

Sputtering, half-frozen, and trembling—with Robert's dripping face close to hers.

"Of all the lame-brained idiots," he was gasping. "Why in the hell didn't you just let go of it?" As she continued to stare at him stupidly, he brought the blue bag to the surface for an instant with his free hand. "What did you plan to do, for god's sake?" he continued angrily. "Walk ashore on the bottom or just stay down there and drown?"

Julie knew better than to argue. It was beyond her capabilities for one thing. All she could manage just then was to grab onto one of the ferry's inner tubes which had providentially floated over beside her. She laid her head on it with a heartfelt sigh—like someone coming home—and gently passed out.

TEN

The rest of that day would always be fogged in Julie's mind. There were parts that came back with clarity—the less painful parts, which was probably nature's way of handling human frailty.

She remembered the trip back across the lake to Parapet in disjointed snatches. The first was when she woke up in the stern of the ferry and found Robert keeping watch over her. Her clothes were still soggy and sticking to her but it was no hardship to wear them in the soaring heat.

She was far more concerned about Dane's whereabouts and Robert correctly interpreted her worried expression when she opened her eyes. "Hamill isn't here," he said brusquely, putting an arm around her shoulders and helping her to sit up by the rail so she could feel the breeze off the water. "Don't give him another thought. They took him in custody and radioed for a police launch to pick him up."

"I'm glad of that," Julie said faintly. Her expression was still puzzled as she stared around the empty stern of the ferry. "Where's Mila?"

"Back on the island along with Dane and that burly crewman who went over with us this morning. He was part of the local constabulary that she'd recruited."

Julie shook a dazed head. "*She'd* recruited! I don't understand. And where's the blue bag?"

"Mila's standing guard over it until she can return it to the Taiwan authorities. Believe me, it would take a whole tribe of Batak witch doctors to get it away from her this time." Robert's features softened after a look at Julie's white face. "Forget about it now—it's all behind us. I'll explain the whole thing after we board the *Mamiri* tonight."

"How can we do that?" She closed her eyes as she tried to remember. "We're still miles from the coast."

"We'll fly on to Sibolga by charter plane today and come back here to see the scenery another time. Right now you need some of the creature comforts." His firm mouth slanted in an appealing grin. "I'd hate to have my wife return from her honeymoon looking like a basket case."

Julie shook her head again, sure that her reason had stayed at the bottom of Lake Toba. "But this isn't a honeymoon. It's a business trip—you said so."

His arm tightened on her fiercely. "Look! Will you forget about what I said then? Just trust me now—at least until we get back aboard ship."

Julie looked at him, the aftereffects of her near-drowning still evident in her parchment cheeks and shadowed eyes. "Of course, I trust you—you know I do. I have all along," she said simply. "That's the trouble."

"I'm not sure I like the way you put it," he began, and then his voice softened, "but I can see your point. Tonight we'll straighten things out aboard the *Mamiri.*"

Julie was content to go along with that. She moved like an automaton later as he helped her to change clothes at the hotel before they were driven to the Parapet airstrip where they eventually boarded a small plane. She dozed in the hot air of the cabin for most of the flight, aware only of the unending dark green Sumatran jungle below them as they flew south across the big island.

The port town of Sibolga had little to recommend it for beauty except for the welcome sight of the *Mamiri* in the middle of the harbor when they arrived in late afternoon.

There was a tender waiting at dockside to lighter them out to the ship, and ten minutes later, Julie was walking up the metal gangway toward Jon Barnes's tall figure at the top of it.

Robert didn't allow her time for more than a brief greeting before he shepherded her along to their suite. He started running water for her bath while she still stood in the middle of the bedroom, looking wearily around her. "You'll feel better after you get cleaned up and have something to eat," he announced briskly. "I'll go make arrangements to have dinner served in here."

She rebelled at that. "I'm not going to play invalid any longer."

"Who said anything about treating you like an invalid? I just thought you might appreciate a little privacy after all you've been through. I know I would."

"You mean you're eating in here, too?" She stared at him, wide-eyed.

"You'd better believe it. Remember what I said about getting you a book on seduction?"

"Vaguely," she replied, trying to hide her confusion. "We both said a lot of silly things."

"Not so silly," he said calmly, as he opened the door. "I've just decided you'd do better with private lessons instead."

She watched with a stupefied expression as the door swung shut behind him. Then she turned and slowly made her way into the bathroom, wondering if this was really happening or whether she was suffering from delayed shock.

Dinner helped to restore a measure of reality. George, beaming hugely at their return, delivered it to their sitting room on two trays about the time the *Mamiri* lifted anchor and set sail for Java.

Julie turned from the window where she'd been watching a vivid sunset which looked like molten gold across the horizon. "It's wonderful to be back aboard," she told Robert when they were alone again. "Like finding a safe harbor after a storm." She smiled apologetically. "As the saying goes."

He smiled back at her. "When you add fair weather and roast beef for dinner, it's not only wonderful—it's a blooming miracle!" He sat down across the table and picked up his fork. "I didn't want you to suffer from withdrawal symptoms though, so I arranged for a special dessert."

"What do you mean?"

He gestured toward her tray. "Rice pudding—that way you can keep in practice."

It wasn't until later, when the dinner trays had been returned to the pantry and they were sitting companionably drinking coffee while watching darkness cover the smooth sea, that Julie brought up the subject they'd been avoiding. She turned to look at Robert, lounging on the divan as he watched the wake of bow waves. He'd changed before dinner into faded blue denims but there was nothing casual about his manner or his glance when she'd encountered it over the dinner table.

She tried to subdue the tension in her own voice as she said, "You can stop treating me with kid gloves now and tell me what happened today."

Robert shifted on the divan to face her more squarely. "Before or after you went to sleep on that inner tube?"

"I'll never forget what happened before it—thanks to your stepping in at the right moment." She wrinkled her nose as she realized what she'd just said. "What an awful pun—I didn't mean it."

"Stepping in at the right moment . . ." Robert muttered, shaking his head. "I think there are still some drafts in your attic. Let's have the confessional another time."

"No way. I want to get it over with." She put her coffee cup down on the table for emphasis. "Did you know that Dane had my name on that miserable blue bag all the time? He told Lukie to put it in dead storage here on the ship when we came aboard at Okinawa."

"That's what Mila reported. I talked to her on the phone after we'd changed clothes at the hotel in Parapet. More coffee?"

"No, thanks." Julie kept her glance lowered, ostensibly engrossed in smoothing a tiny wrinkle from the skirt of her silk shantung robe. "I'd like to hear more about Mila. You didn't tell me that she was a policewoman."

"That's because she asked me not to. She briefed me on the situation at the Marden office in Singapore. Apparently, the Taiwan authorities didn't have any real evidence against Dane, but he was a prime suspect in the thefts. That's why they assigned Mila to keep an eye on him. She was good-looking enough to allay any suspicion on his part."

"Policewomen don't usually come with her measurements," Julie acknowledged. "Not as a general rule."

A slow grin creased his face. "The rule still applies. She's not a real policewoman but an official in the Internal Affairs section of the Taiwan government."

"Then it was a lot of malarky about you knowing her when she was a beauty queen?"

Robert's grin broadened at the evident relief in her voice. "No, that part was true. I knew her a few years ago—but not very well," he finished diplomatically.

Julie's eyes flashed then. "And you had the nerve to object to Geoff Clarke!"

"That's putting it mildly. I wanted to wring his neck—right after I'd finished wringing yours," Robert admitted. "Do you want to fight about that now or shall we get back to Dane's blue bag?"

"The blue bag," she said, deciding that it wasn't apt to cause so much trouble. "I still don't know what was in it."

"That was no reason for clutching it to your bosom at the bottom of Samosir harbor," Robert said, sounding just as angry on that subject. "I had to pry it out of your hands when I found you."

"I'd forgotten that I even had it. Dane scared me to death when he came after me on the pier. The expression on his face . . ." She broke off, shuddering at the memory.

"Forget about it. Mr. Hamill is sitting in an Indonesian jail at the moment and they don't feature modern conveniences. He'll have lots of time to repent his sins before he's extradited to

Taiwan. I have an idea the police there will take a very narrow view of his absconding with their national treasures."

"You mean that's what was in the bag?"

"A big part of it. According to Mila, he was carrying around three choice pieces of the National Museum's cinnabar collection. One was a sixteenth-century plate decorated with a pair of dragons from the Ming dynasty that's almost priceless. Fortunately, all the pieces were in padded waterproof bags, so they weren't damaged by the dunking."

"Thank heavens for that." There was relief in Julie's voice but a frown still marred her forehead. "Why on earth didn't somebody search his things before this?"

"Because they didn't have any real evidence at the time he skipped out to Okinawa. I suspect that he needed a refuge until the furor and publicity over the thefts died down. And what better place than an American freighter plying international waters? Especially when he had a logical excuse for being aboard."

"And the *Mamiri* people wouldn't go through our luggage—"

"Well, they certainly didn't go through yours," Robert agreed. "That's one reason Dane had the blue bag tagged with your name. It must have been an awful shock to him when he saw Lukie putting it ashore after we docked in Sumatra. He'd probably hoped to get hold of it before we came back to the ship."

"That's why he was so upset when I threatened to stay aboard and not go overland with you," she said, thinking back. "Right after I mentioned it to Dane, the stairway was booby-trapped. Do you think it was his way of persuading me not to linger around?"

"Very likely."

"I suppose I should be glad that he didn't use a wrench, but maybe the wrench supply was exhausted after that 'near miss' on the gangway in Okinawa. At least now I know that was an accident." She smiled ruefully. "Not that it would have been much consolation if the wrench had connected with my head."

"That thought had occurred to me," Robert kept his tone light although his expression was sober as he studied her pale complexion. The lamplight served to burnish the golden highlights in her hair, but it also revealed the smudges under her gray-blue eyes that remained as mute evidence of her ordeal. At least her return to the security of the freighter had helped to dissipate her fragile air, and he was happy to see she was fast returning to normal. Normal enough that he could now safely tease her about the past. "Why in the hell didn't you want to go ashore with me in Sumatra?" he asked, although he had a very good idea.

"Because you'd been acting like a perfect horror ever since you'd come aboard in Singapore," she told him tartly, confirming his suspicions. "How do you think I felt when I saw Mila clinging to you down on the pier?"

"I hope the same way *I* felt when I saw you alongside our prime suspect by the rail," he countered.

She made a helpless gesture. "Yes, but you hadn't wanted me to come along in the first place. If it hadn't been for your hand . . ." Her voice dropped as she shot him a brooding glance. "I'm beginning to wonder about the doctor's report on it."

"It's taken you long enough," Robert said, grinning.

When he started to move closer, Julie shook her head, "Wait a minute, you're going too fast for me."

"Okay, my love, but sooner or later we'll get to it," he told her, calmly sitting back. "Where were we?"

"Lukie had unloaded the blue bag in Belawan." It was the only thing she could think to say after Robert had called her "my love" in that casual way.

"And Dane decided suddenly to make the overland journey with us," Robert went on. "To keep an eye on his property. Afterward, the heat and discomfort gave him a perfect excuse to take off on his own. It also made Mila desperate because he was going to slip out of the net. That's what she wanted to talk to me about last night at the hotel."

Julie bit her lip in chagrin as she realized that Mila had been talking about Dane in that telephone conversation she'd overheard. "I thought she was up to her neck in skullduggery and you were the object of it."

"I wondered what was in your mind at the time." Robert started to chuckle. "There was frustration all around. Dane couldn't get to the luggage in the van because Lukie drove it off to the suburbs, Mila was trying to secure an Indonesian policeman on the lake ferry because she didn't have any authority in Sumatra, and you . . ." He paused, trying not to laugh.

"Acted like an idiot," she replied bitterly.

"I wouldn't say so
lack of it—put the c
years." Robert's voice
damn about Dane's crin
hell never forgive him
night."

Julie lifted her palms t
"Oh, please—you don't hav
mured unhappily. "I reme
forced into this ridiculous
place. If my grandfather hadn't issued that ultimatum—"

"Stop right there," Robert interrupted. "I saw
your grandfather before I flew to Singapore."

"You saw him?" she whispered, wide-eyed.
"But why?"

"Because I wanted to shake his hand and thank
him for giving me an excuse to get your name on
a marriage license. If you'll remember, things had
gotten a little out of control at that point."

"You were furious with me," she said flatly.

"Damned right I was. Ever since I'd found
you draped in Geoff Clarke's arms. I'd been taking it slow and easy in getting to know you—doing the courtship routine by the book—then you
flaunted that idiot in my face."

"Will you listen!" she cut in desperately. "That
kiss was Geoff's idea, not mine. He probably even
kissed the cleaning ladies on his way out of the
building that day. There was no excuse for you to
fly into the boughs over it. Besides, what about
Miss Flynn? You weren't long in finding a substi-
tute to make you feel better . . ." She broke off
then. She had to because Robert had moved
swiftly over and pulled her to her feet, catching

erful embrace that her lips were
...s tanned throat.

...back to normal," he said happily, not
... his grip by one iota. "Now—if you'll
...mise not to hit me, I'll apologize for dragging
...mogene in to make you jealous. As a matter of
fact, I'll do more than that." His hands moved upward over her back and around to cup the gentle
curve of her breasts, letting her feel the warmth
of his hands through the thin material of her robe.
"It's been the very devil trying to act like we
weren't on a honeymoon," he muttered, his lips
nuzzling the soft hollow under her ear. "I
couldn't be in the same room with you without
wanting my hands on you—to touch you—to do a
hell of a lot more than that." He pushed aside the
lapels of her robe and she trembled as his fingers
moved possessively over her, awakening desire everywhere he touched.

Instinctively she reached up and pulled his
head down so his mouth could cover hers. He was
gentle at first until he felt her response and need.
Then his lips hardened, urgently parting hers
with answering demand.

Darkness had completely shrouded the calm sea
when he switched off the lights, letting the pale
gleam of moonlight guide them to the open bedroom door.

That open door was the first thing Julie saw the
next morning as she was awakened by a determined knocking from the hallway. The next thing
she noticed was the travel clock on the bedside
table which showed six-thirty on the dial.

"Robert, darling—wake up!" she whispered. "There's someone at the door. Did you leave a call for early coffee?"

A sleepy groan came from the man lying beside her. "Oh, lord, I forgot to cancel it when we came back aboard." He pushed down the sheet and swung his legs to the floor. "Where did I leave my robe?"

"In the closet. At least, you didn't have it last night. I remember that very well."

"I hope that isn't all you remember." He turned to grin at her over a broad shoulder and then yanked the robe from a closet hook as the knocking started again. "Okay, okay, I'm coming," he called out.

As he disappeared into the sitting room Julie remembered her own conspicuous lack of attire and slid hastily down under the covers. She pretended to be asleep as she heard George talking to Robert and the rattle of china as a tray was deposited in the other room. Then there were retreating footsteps and the sound of the hall door being closed.

She was sitting up in bed again when Robert came back to the bedroom. "We forgot to muss up the covers on that other bed," she announced as he shed his robe on a chair and walked toward her. "What will George think?"

"Who knows?" Robert said calmly, getting back in bed and pulling her close. "But now I can understand his parting remark." Robert's voice was muffled as he searched for the soft resting place he'd occupied earlier.

"Stop talking in riddles, you brute." Julie's ultimatum wasn't particularly effective since she was gently smoothing the back of his head at the time. "What did George say to you?"

"Just that we needn't bother to come to breakfast if it wasn't convenient. He promised to leave some food in the pantry. I always did appreciate a practical man." Robert deposited a light kiss for emphasis. "Don't you, my love?" He felt Julie's soft laughter and pushed up on an elbow, letting his glance linger on her loveliness. "Aren't you going to answer me?" he teased as she colored under his appreciative gaze.

"A practical man wouldn't be asking questions at a time like this," his wife reminded him, using her finger for emphasis as she gently traced his brow. "Of course, if you'd rather discuss it more sensibly, we can get up now and have our coffee. Afterward, there should be plenty of time before breakfast to resolve the finer points of our future policy . . ."

Her conversation ceased abruptly as Robert demonstrated there was no need for further discussion, showing a remarkable aptitude in resolving those finer points she'd mentioned. He also proved conclusively that he could handle any small developments that they might anticipate in their future dealings.

The coffee stayed where it was.

And at lunchtime, George wasn't surprised to find the pantry still undisturbed. He would have bet on it.

About the Author

Glenna Finley is a native of Washington State. She earned her degree from Stanford University in Russian Studies and in Speech and Dramatic Arts, with emphasis on radio.

After a stint in radio and publicity work in Seattle, she went to New York City to work for NBC as a producer in its international division. In addition, she worked with the "March of Time" and *Life* magazine.

As a producer, she had her own show about activities in Manhattan, a show that was broadcast to England. The programs were similar to those of the "Voice of America."

Though her life in New York was exciting, she eventually returned to the Northwest where she married. Currently residing in Seattle with her husband, Donald Witte, and their son, she loves to travel, and draws heavily on her travels and experiences for the novels that have been published. Her books for NAL have sold several million copies.

Big Bestsellers from SIGNET

☐ **LOVE ME TOMORROW** by Robert H. Rimmer.
(#E8385—$2.50)*

☐ **NEVER CALL IT LOVE** by Veronica Jason. (#J8343—$1.95)*

☐ **BLACK DAWN** by Christopher Nicole. (#E8342—$2.25)*

☐ **CARIBEE** by Christopher Nicole. (#J7945—$1.95)

☐ **THE DEVIL'S OWN** by Christopher Nicole. (#J7256—$1.95)

☐ **MISTRESS OF DARKNESS** by Christopher Nicole.
(#J7782—$1.95)

☐ **THE WICKED GUARDIAN** by Vanessa Gray.
(#E8390—$1.75)*

☐ **SONG OF SOLOMON** by Toni Morrison. (#E8340—$2.50)*

☐ **RAPTURE'S MISTRESS** by Gimone Hall. (#E8422—$2.25)*

☐ **PRESIDENTIAL EMERGENCY** by Walter Stovall.
(#E8371—$2.25)*

☐ **GIFTS OF LOVE** by Charlotte Vale Allen. (#J8388—$1.95)*

☐ **BELLADONNA** by Erica Lindley. (#J8387—$1.95)*

☐ **THE BRACKENROYD INHERITANCE** by Erica Lindley.
(#W6795—$1.50)

☐ **THE DEVIL IN CRYSTAL** by Erica Lindley. (#E7643—$1.75)

☐ **THE GODFATHER** by Mario Puzo. (#E8508—$2.50)*

☐ **KRAMER VERSUS KRAMER** by Avery Corman.
(#E8282—$2.50)

☐ **JOURNEY ON THE WIND** by Kay McDonald.
(#J8547—$1.95)

☐ **VISION OF THE EAGLE** by Kay McDonald. (#J8284—$1.95)

☐ **HOMICIDE ZONE FOUR** by Nick Christian.
(#J8285—$1.95)*

☐ **CLEARED FOR THE APPROACH** by F. Lee Bailey with
John Greenya. (#E8286—$2.50)*

* Price slightly higher in Canada

Other SIGNET Bestsellers You'll Enjoy

☐ **CRESSIDA by Clare Darcy.** (#E8287—$1.75)*

☐ **DANIEL MARTIN by John Fowles.** (#E8249—$2.95)

☐ **THE EBONY TOWER by John Fowles.** (#E8254—$2.50)

☐ **THE FRENCH LIEUTENANT'S WOMAN by John Fowles.**
(#E8535—$2.50)

☐ **RIDE THE BLUE RIBAND by Rosalind Laker.**
(#J8252—$1.95)*

☐ **MISTRESS OF OAKHURST—Book II by Walter Reed Johnson.** (#J8253—$1.95)

☐ **OAKHURST—Book I by Walter Reed Johnson.**
(#J7874—$1.95)

☐ **THE SILVER FALCON by Evelyn Anthony.** (#E8211—$2.25)

☐ **I, JUDAS by Taylor Caldwell and Jess Stearn.**
(#E8212—$2.50)*

☐ **THE RAGING WINDS OF HEAVEN by June Shiplett.**
(#J8213—$1.95)*

☐ **THE TODAY SHOW by Robert Metz.** (#E8214—$2.25)

☐ **BLOCKBUSTER by Stephen Barlay.** (#E8111—$2.25)*

☐ **BALLET! by Tom Murphy.** (#E8112—$2.25)*

☐ **THE LADY SERENA by Jeanne Duval.** (#E8163—$2.25)*

☐ **LOVING STRANGERS by Jack Mayfield.** (#J8216—$1.95)*

☐ **BORN TO WIN by Muriel James and Dorothy Jongeward.**
(#E8169—$2.50)*

☐ **BORROWED PLUMES by Roseleen Milne.** (#E8113—$1.75)

☐ **ROGUE'S MISTRESS by Constance Gluyas.**
(#E8339—$2.25)

☐ **SAVAGE EDEN by Constance Gluyas.** (#E8338—$2.25)

☐ **WOMAN OF FURY by Constance Gluyas.** (#E8075—$2.25)*

* Price slightly higher in Canada

Have You Read These Bestsellers from SIGNET?

- ☐ **BEYOND THE MALE MYTH** by Anthony Pietropinto, M.D., and Jacqueline Simenauer. (#E8076—$2.50)
- ☐ **CRAZY LOVE: An Autobiographical Account of Marriage and Madness** by Phyllis Naylor. (#J8077—$1.95)
- ☐ **THE PSYCHOPATHIC GOD—ADOLF HITLER** by Robert G. L. Waite. (#E8078—$2.95)
- ☐ **THE SERIAL** by Cyra McFadden. (#J8080—$1.95)
- ☐ **THE RULING PASSION** by Shaun Herron. (#E8042—$2.25)
- ☐ **CONSTANTINE CAY** by Catherine Dillon. (#J8307—$1.95)
- ☐ **WHITE FIRES BURNING** by Catherine Dillon. (#J8281—$1.95)
- ☐ **THE WHITE KHAN** by Catherine Dillon. (#J8043—$1.95)*
- ☐ **THE MASTERS WAY TO BEAUTY** by George Masters and Norma Lee Browning. (#E8044—$2.25)
- ☐ **KID ANDREW CODY AND JULIE SPARROW** by Tony Curtis. (#E8010—$2.25)*
- ☐ **WINTER FIRE** by Susannah Leigh. (#E8011—$2.25)*
- ☐ **THE MESSENGER** by Mona Williams. (#J8012—$1.95)
- ☐ **FEAR OF FLYING** by Erica Jong. (#E7970—$2.25)
- ☐ **HOW TO SAVE YOUR OWN LIFE** by Erica Jong. (#E7959—$2.50)*

* Price slightly higher in Canada